I've travelled the world twice over,
Met the famous: saints and sinners,
Poets and artists, kings and queens,
Old stars and hopeful beginners,
I've been where no-one's been before,
Learned secrets from writers and cooks
All with one library ticket
To the wonderful world of books.

© JANICE JAMES.

VOW OF PENANCE

On the Cornish moor where Sister Joan lives with other Sisters of the Daughters of Compassion, a shadowy figure is stalking the night, slashing trees. When Father Malone's housekeeper is found dead, suicide is the verdict — but Sister Joan and her old friend, Detective Sergeant Mill, think otherwise. When Sister Joan is sent to the presbytery to work as temporary housekeeper, the stage is set for a race against time to find the truth before the stalker turns the season of penance into a season of blood.

VERONICA BLACK

◆

VOW OF PENANCE

Complete and Unabridged

ULVERSCROFT
Leicester

First published in Great Britain in 1994 by
Robert Hale Limited
London

First Large Print Edition
published July 1995
by arrangement with
Robert Hale Limited
London

British Library CIP Data

Black, Veronica
Vow of penance.—Large print ed.—
Ulverscroft large print series: mystery
I. Title
823.914 [F]

ISBN 0–7089–3326–2

Published by
F. A. Thorpe (Publishing) Ltd.
Anstey, Leicestershire
Set by Words & Graphics Ltd.
Anstey, Leicestershire
Printed and bound in Great Britain by
T. J. Press (Padstow) Ltd., Padstow, Cornwall

This book is printed on acid-free paper

1

"FEBRUARY," said Sister Joan, scowling at the melted slush in the yard, "is the longest month in the year."

"I know exactly what you mean," Sister Teresa said ruefully. "You know I'm sure that winters used to be warmer down in Cornwall."

"It's all because of the ozone layer." Sister Perpetua came briskly into the kitchen. "Not to mention the stuff they're flinging up into the atmosphere!"

"I thought it had to do with the tilt of the earth changing," Sister Teresa said.

"Has recreation started already?" a voice enquired from the doorway. Three white-veiled heads turned towards the purple-habited figure of the prioress. Mother Dorothy, Sister Joan thought, was certainly not a prioress who sat in her parlour and issued orders from a distance. Mother Dorothy was far more likely to be met with as she bristled about the convent, running her fingertips along the polished balustrade of the staircase the better to check for dust, poking about in the pantry to make sure that food wasn't being wasted, turning up unexpectedly when three of her nuns had relaxed into a strictly unofficial chat.

"I'm afraid I began it," Sister Joan said.

Mother Dorothy's bespectacled countenance remained entirely unsurprised as she heard the admission. In Mother Dorothy's opinion Sister Joan seemed to begin most trains of events that ended with the rule being, not actually broken, but certainly bent.

"Our rule provides for our speaking of matters connected with our work or with spiritual matters," the prioress said. "We have a period of recreation every evening during which we may converse on more varied topics. It sets no very good example to Sister Teresa who must soon draw apart for her final period of preparation for her full entry into the community."

Sister Teresa, marked out from her grey-habited companions by a blue habit, said earnestly, "Forgive me, Reverend Mother, but the tilting of the earth could be described as a theological problem, don't you think?"

"Not in this Order," Mother Dorothy said quellingly.

And that, thought Sister Joan, refraining from exchanging glances with Sister Perpetua, was that. Mother Dorothy had spoken. From henceforth discussion of the ozone layer and the part science was playing in creating the greenhouse effect were not subjects to be discussed in the Cornwall House of the Order of Daughters of Compassion. The Order was neither ancient nor large but the authority of each prioress over her sisters during her term of office was undisputed. The rule of the Order was followed by everybody but the way in which it was interpreted varied greatly.

"I have an announcement to make at supper," Mother Dorothy said, in the manner of an adult offering a small treat to a scolded child, "so it would be appreciated if the meal could be absolutely punctual."

She nodded her head and went out;

Sister Teresa went to the oven and started taking out the baked potatoes, her cheeks still rather flushed. There would be melted cheese and chopped cabbage to go with the potatoes and an apple tart to follow. The nuns followed a vegetarian regime which certainly did their skins no harm, Sister Joan mused, taking a final unauthorized look through the window before she began piling up the plates. She wondered what the announcement was going to be about. Something out of the common run to judge from Mother's tone.

"I'll get my old ladies settled," Sister Perpetua said and went out, treading lightly on her large, flat feet.

The two oldest members of the convent, Sisters Gabrielle and Mary Concepta, were both well into their eighties. Sister Mary Concepta went through her days in a state of gentle bewilderment; Sister Gabrielle was of tougher mettle, sharp tongued, quick witted, endlessly tolerant.

Sister Teresa banged the gong, as if, Sister Joan thought, anyone needed reminding in the middle of Lent that it

4

was suppertime. During Lent the usual breakfast of coffee, a slice of bread and a piece of fruit was still eaten, but the normal lunch of soup and a salad sandwich was reduced merely to soup. By suppertime even Sister Hilaria, Mistress of Novices, had worked up an appetite.

Here came Sister Hilaria now, large, slow moving, with the somewhat prominent eyes of the born mystic, shepherding her two charges before her like an absentminded shepherdess with two straying pink sheep. The garments worn by the postulants were designed to knock any foolish vanity right out of their shaven heads. Shapeless pink smocks hung from neck to ankles and large white bonnets cut off their side view. After their two years in the postulancy they moved, like Sister Teresa, into the novitiate, permitted to grow their hair a couple of inches, to wear a blue, belted habit and short white veil. And now Sister Teresa was due to move into the year of silence and soul searching before her final year of initiation. It was small wonder that new vocations were scarce.

"Better one good vocation than half a dozen halfhearted ones," Sister Gabrielle had once commented when the subject arose.

Despite their identical clothes and attitudes, heads bent, hands clasped at waist level, Sister Marie and Sister Elizabeth could never be mistaken for twins. The latter never raised her voice above a respectful whisper, guarded whatever feelings she might have had behind a settled blandness of expression, and not only gave the impression of docility but was, Sister Joan suspected, genuinely so. Sister Marie, on the other hand, had retained a decided twinkle in her eyes and a mobile mouth that seemed always on the verge of laughter.

The gong clanged again and she hastily picked up the pile of plates, thinking that it would save a lot of fetching and carrying if the refectory had been situated on the ground floor near the kitchen. But the house hadn't been built originally as a convent but as a handsome home for wealthy landowners. Not all the conventual austerity in the world could alter the sweep of the staircase as it rose out of the wide entrance hall or the delicate moulding of the fanlights and ceilings.

She carried the tray carefully into the short passage, past the dispensary where Sister Perpetua did amazing things with herbs, past the infirmary where the two old ladies were eating their supper, up the wide stairs into the huge apartment where girls with flowers in their hair had once danced but was now divided into two with the dining area immediately within the double doors and the recreation area beyond.

The rest of the community with the exception of Sister Gabrielle and Sister Mary Concepta stood behind their backless stools. Sister Joan set the plates down on the serving trolley and stood with Sister Teresa ready to serve the rest. As acting lay sister she and her assistant would eat later. She had been acting lay sister ever since the Authority had closed down the little school on the moor where she had taught local children, and while she appreciated the freedom of being allowed to drive the ancient car into town to do the weekly shopping she had not yet learned to relish chilly, congealed food.

"Sisters, I have only one announcement to make this evening." Mother Dorothy broke the silence crisply. "Father Malone is to take a sabbatical for a year."

Within the veils and bonnets of the assembled company expressions were surprised and disappointed. Father Malone was not the most spiritual or the most learned of clerics, but he was a comfortable and familiar figure in his rusty cassock with a vast muffler wrapped round his neck in winter and a yellowing panama hat on his head in summer. Unlike Father Stephens with his melodious voice and degree in theology Father Malone was quite unable to indulge in finely tuned philosophical argument. He merely knew right from wrong, praised the former and shook his head over the latter, indulged himself in a spot of innocent flirtation when he came to the convent and kept a supply of wine gums for the smaller members of his congregation.

"Father Malone," Mother Dorothy was continuing, "is to spend several months in spiritual retreat before undertaking a tour of holy places in Europe and the Middle East. It is a wonderful opportunity for him so, while we must inevitably regret his absence, we can take pleasure in the fact that he will be enjoying a rich and varied experience, and, of course Father Stephens will be remaining here to administer the Holy Sacraments and deal with our spiritual problems."

There was slightly less than wholehearted enthusiasm in her voice. Not even Mother Dorothy could convince herself that Father Stephens was an adequate substitute. He looked like a handsome young bishop, towards which eminent position he was doubtless headed, and his sermons were laced with obscure quotations, but he wore his goodness like a top hat instead of like a shabbily comfortable cardigan.

"Let us say Grace," Mother Dorothy said, and recited it briskly.

Usually the sisters took it in turns to read aloud from an improving book during supper but this being Lent the meal was eaten in silence. Not until the rest of the community had filed through to recreation could Sister Joan and Sister Teresa eat their own meal, then clear everything away and take it down to the kitchen to be washed up. They ate quickly and silently, aware of the low murmur of voices behind the double doors. The departure of Father Malone would be the chief topic of conversation as they occupied themselves with the handicrafts that kept hands from being idle while their tongues wagged.

Not until they were rinsing out the tea towels did Sister Teresa permit herself to say, "I'm sure Father Malone will have a wonderful time but he'll be sorely missed here, don't you think, Sister Joan?"

"He'll be going to Jerusalem and Rome," Sister Joan said. She would have been less than human if there hadn't been a tinge of envy in her tone.

"Lourdes, La Salette, Assisi, Padua — all the holy shrines," Sister Teresa agreed. He would see the Chagall stained-glass windows in the great synogogue, the work of Michaelangelo, Fra Angelico, Botticelli — Sister Joan checked her train of thought sharply. Father Malone's taste ran to pink-cheeked plaster Madonnas and nice little souvenirs he could send to his old mother back in Ireland.

"Perhaps someone will come to assist Father Stephens," she said aloud. "His parish is rather far flung after all."

It was spread across the moor, encompassing farm, modern estate sprawl and the Romany camp as well as several small villages and the convent itself. Father Malone was always trying to catch up with himself as he hurtled round in a car almost as ancient as the one the convent owned, part of his problem being that he could never confine himself to a formal visit of twenty minutes but must waste time in talking over problems, listening to strings of complaints, and telling long, rambling stories to the children who came flying from every direction when his horn sounded.

"That would be nice," Sister Teresa said, wiping her hands neatly.

Outside a series of barks announced the arrival of Alice, ready for scraps. The Alsatian puppy, pressed on the community by Detective Sergeant Mill, had never succeeded in learning that scraps in a convent were scarce, the plates being scraped clean at every meal. Sister Joan glanced at her companion.

"Would you like to give Alice her supper?" she asked.

"Thank you, Sister." The other's face brightened as she went to admit Alice who had started scratching on the door with her feathery paws.

Alice's official function was to train as a guard for the community, a precaution that Detective Sergeant Mill had insisted upon after the events of the previous autumn.[1] Those events were never mentioned but the presence of Alice was a reminder that even amid the rich beauties of the moor danger could lurk. Mother Dorothy had considered the keeping of a dog unsuitable for cloistered women but had agreed to it on condition that Alice was kept in her place. Alice, who clearly believed she owned the entire convent and only permitted human beings there as a favour, spent her days working out how to get the better of Mother

[1] See Vow Of Obedience

Prioress whose position she had instantly recognized even though she wasn't willing to submit to her authority. Now, let in by one of the lesser humans, she pranced about the black-clad ankles before trotting to her bowl to inspect the contents.

Sister Joan smiled to herself as she closed the door behind her. As acting lay sister she was not required to attend the evening recreation that was sandwiched between supper and the final benediction of the day. This was not a great deprivation as far as she was concerned since conversation centred on the mundane. Instead she relished the half-hour or so when she was free to follow her own inclinations.

Usually she put on her cloak and took a brisk walk in the gardens but the darkness of this inhospitable month was creeping over moor and wall, and she went instead through the door at the right of the entrance hall which led past the parlour and the visitors' parlour into the chapel. Modern innovations had no place here. There were still candles flaring on their spiked sconces and a small organ with no electronic additions. Sister Joan

13

dipped her knee to the altar, reached up to give the statue of the Madonna a friendly pat and went up the stairs that wound up to the library and storerooms above.

Sister David was in charge of the library and ran it with quiet efficiency, but the storerooms were a glorious jumble of old furniture, discarded ornaments, books, piles of newspapers and magazines going back fifty years. It was to these latter that Sister Joan took herself, switching on the one light bulb and carrying a pile, their edges tattered and their print beginning to fade, over to the table. Though spare time was something of which she, in common with everybody else in the convent, had very little, there were always spare moments which could be filled up with some useful and interesting activity. She had decided a couple of weeks before that a history of the district might well prove of interest to future generations and was now engaged in snipping out items of local news which could eventually be mounted in a scrapbook.

"Sister David generally undertakes the research projects here," Mother Dorothy had observed when Sister Joan had applied to her for permission.

"Research into the saints," Sister Joan had countered. "Her series of stories for children requires a lot of effort on her part, as well as the library to run and her secretarial duties."

"Very well." Having considered the matter Mother Dorothy gave her judgement in her usual brisk fashion. "In your spare time, and provided it doesn't interfere with either your religious life or your secular duties then I see no reason why you should not embark on this task. I am sure it isn't merely an excuse to have a good browse through all the local scandals."

Behind her spectacles her eyes had held a disconcerting twinkle. Mother Dorothy, Sister Joan thought, carefully scissoring out an account of A.R.P. work and clipping it to the 1940 pile, knew her charges very well.

The fob watch pinned to her belt warned her that recreation would soon be drawing to a close. Sister Hilaria had already returned with her pink-smocked charges to the old dower house at the far side of the abandoned tennis courts which served as the postulancy.

'Trees damaged on local estate' ran the next headline. Twenty years old, Sister Joan noted, and scanned the item hastily. A large number of trees had been attacked by someone with an axe who had lopped off branches and left deep cuts in the trunks. Mindless vandalism and the only reason for preserving the cutting was that the trees had formed part of the estate on which the convent stood. It had not then become a convent but was still in private hands. Nevertheless it was worth keeping. She cut round it, clipped it to the requisite pile, and rose, switching off the light, making her way past shrouded packing cases to the tiny washbasin where she could rinse her hands before descending into chapel for the final benediction that heralded the grand silence.

The community filed in, heads bent, hands candled. Against the walls their shadows made Gothic shapes. At such times their separate personalities were merged into the image of devotion and dedication that marked every religious.

16

Delicate seeming Sister Martha who did the bulk of the gardening singlehanded and still looked as if a breeze might waft her away became, like the large boned Sister Perpetua, merely another facet in the diamond bright virtues of the Order.

"We will pray tonight for Father Malone's happy and holy sabbatical and his safe return to us," Mother Dorothy said, rising. "Let us also pray for Father Stephens whose work load will be greatly increased during this coming year."

Prayers over there was a brief period of meditation before the recitation of the rosary began. Sister Joan bowed her head, lips tracing the familiar words, thoughts of the great art treasures that Father Malone would have the chance to see firmly banished. Envy had no place in the nature of a Daughter of Compassion. However a touch of wistfulness remained.

"Sisters, go in peace." Mother Dorothy's voice sounded calm and sure amid the shadows cast by the flickering candle flames.

Did the prioress still harbour worldly desires? Did she, in some corner of her disciplined heart, regret never having seen or done something or other? Kneeling for the blessing, the light sprinkling of holy water, Sister Joan considered it unlikely.

She waited until the last of the community had filed out, received Mother Dorothy's final goodnight nod, and began her rounds. Candles to be snuffed, missals to be piled on the shelf, doors and windows to be locked and checked. At her heels Sister Teresa pattered silently. In the kitchen Alice lay curled in her basket by the stove. Night came down gently over the convent.

The final smiling nod exchanged and the two sisters separated, each entering one of the two lay cells off the kitchen. Long practice had accustomed Sister Joan to undressing, washing hands and face and cleaning her teeth without the aid of a mirror. On the rare occasions when she caught a glimpse of herself in a mirror she was always agreeably surprised to discover that she looked about ten years younger than her actual age, her cheeks rosy and her dark blue eyes marked only by the faintest laughter lines. She slipped the long white nightdress over her head, ran a comb through her short, shining blue-black hair, and got into bed, wishing as her hip bones contacted the thin mattress on its wooden base that she was a little more generously endowed with curves. There remained only her private prayers to mouth silently and a last whimper from Alice, chasing tails in her sleep.

Over in the postulancy Sister Hilaria took a final peep at her two sleeping charges and padded down the stairs to check that the door was bolted. She had already checked it or thought she had, but since practical matters were apt to confuse her she always made a point of doing everything twice in case she had forgotten the first time.

When a new lay sister could be found Sister Joan would rejoin the general community and take up her duties as assistant novice mistress. Sister Hilaria smiled at the prospect. Sister Joan was lively and funny and never forgot to lock up or sweep out the cells. With Sister Joan around she could spend more time on the spiritual lives of the two girls in her charge. Sister Hilaria stared vaguely at the door, wondering why she had come downstairs. To check the door had been bolted. Yes, that was it. She turned the handle and was only mildly surprised to find out that the door opened at once. How wise she had been to check twice since it was clear she had neglected to bolt up the first time.

Outside a low wall separated the small building from the old tennis courts. The posts were still there, gleaming faintly as the moon emerged. At the other side of the courts a path wound up through the shrubbery to the walled enclosure with its small cemetery, its flowers, fruit and vegetables. At this month of the year only the holly bushes dotted about on the open ground outside the enclosure wall were leafy, berries still gleaming like scarlet beads against the dark green. Not that one could distinguish colours in the moonlight, Sister Hilaria mused, holding the door ajar, sending good thoughts across to the sisters in the main house. Those who slept deeply or tossed on their thin mattresses would have been astonished to learn how much the unworldly mistress of novices knew about them. Sister Hilaria was never quite sure exactly how many were in the community nor who performed which duties but she knew the essence of each soul, knew who was troubled about some small personal fault, who felt stirrings of rebellion or missed their family in the mundane world. She could recognize evil too, could smell it on the wind before it had made itself manifest.

She could smell it now, far off, faint. Not yet here but coming. For a moment she stood frowning, then with a little shiver she closed and bolted the door.

★ ★ ★

The row of bonsai trees stood on the wide windowsill, each branch, each leaf a perfect miniature. The tiny oak spread itself as proudly as its full-sized brother; the willow created a filigree umbrella over the smooth surface of a tiny pond edged with shards of coloured glass. The hands that moved gently, inexorably, towards the tiny trees held a sharp pruning knife, razor honed. Delicately the tip of the knife sliced into bark and bud, and the lacy filaments of the willow fell and lay like strands of silk on the surface of the tiny pool. There was no sound save the pleased intake of breath as the sap began to trickle down, the despoiled foliage to wither and when the knife was withdrawn only a few branches remained, holding up their dwarfish arms like small penitents pleading for mercy.

2

"HOW the parish will manage when you're away we can't imagine, Father," Sister David said mournfully.

"Everybody will manage very nicely," Father Malone said cheerfully. "There's nobody who's indispensable, you know, and to tell the truth there are those who regard me as a mite old-fashioned in my thinking."

"Not in this convent," Mother Dorothy said.

Mass was over and they were standing in the refectory, eating the bread and fruit and drinking the one cup of coffee which was their staple breakfast while Father Malone chatted about his forthcoming trip.

"We'll be stuck with Father Stephens," Sister Perpetua said.

"What Sister means," said Mother Dorothy, "is that Father Stephens will have a very heavy burden and less time

23

to devote to his various commitments."

Father Malone, who knew very well what Sister Perpetua had meant, threw her a reassuring glance.

"We've been very fortunate," he said. "The bishop is sending a temporary replacement for me during my sabbatical. Father Matthew Timothy is recently ordained and fresh out of the seminary."

Mother Dorothy pursed her lips slightly but gave no other sign of disapproval. In her experience young priests fresh out of the seminary were usually still wet behind the ears and full of bright reforming ideas out of which she considered it her duty to wean them. For the moment, however, she held her peace.

"I shall be assisting at a concelebrated mass in St Peter's on Easter Sunday," Father Malone was saying with shy pleasure. "I'm really overwhelmed by the honour."

"You'll see His Holiness," Sister Katherine said.

"Indeed I will though it's doubtful if His Holiness will see me!" Having chuckled at his own small jest Father Malone shook hands all round, promised to send postcards, and bustled out, flinging the ends of his muffler over his shoulders as he went with the air of an elderly schoolboy let out for half-term.

The normal routine of the conventual day continued. Cells must be swept and the two bathrooms at the end of the upper corridor scoured before the sisters repaired to their respective duties. The Order of the Daughters of Compassion was semi-enclosed, there being some latitude permitted if a nun was required to work beyond the enclosure. At the moment however, with the school closed and Sister Joan undertaking the task of lay sister, nobody needed to leave the grounds apart from Sister David who occasionally sought permission to go to the public library on matters connected with her research. Eventually the series of children's stories she was writing might find a publisher and bring in some much needed revenue. For the rest Sister Martha sold what vegetables were in season after the convent had been supplied and Sister Katherine had a regular list of customers for her exquisite lace and embroidered accessories.

And I, thought Sister Joan, scowling at a washrag, could earn more for the Order if Mother Dorothy would allow me to sell some paintings.

The mother prioress had not, however, suggested that her talents should be put to such practical use. She probably thought that such praise would go to Sister Joan's head. In which belief she was very likely justified, Sister Joan thought ruefully, giving the wash basin a final rinse before she went downstairs to start polishing the entrance hall.

From the passage that led past infirmary and office into the kitchen a voice said with a querulous edge, "So we are to have a new priest inflicted upon us just when I was hoping for some peace and quiet!"

"No you weren't, Sister Gabrielle," Sister Joan said, straightening up. "You loathe peace and quiet. You know you do."

"I like a nice mixture," Sister Gabrielle said placidly. "Do you know anything about this Father Timothy?"

"Only that he's newly ordained."

"Oh dear!" The old nun pulled a wry

face. "That means he'll probably want to jazz up the mass with guitars and amplifiers and things."

"I imagine Mother Dorothy would have something to say about that," Sister Joan said, amused.

"Well, God speed Father Malone anyway," Sister Gabrielle said. "I hope they don't recognize his exceptional qualities in the Vatican or we'll never get him back. When is this new priest arriving?"

"Fairly soon I imagine, Sister. It's a lot of work for Father Stephens to handle all by himself."

"You'd better get on with your polishing then," Sister Gabrielle said.

"Yes, Sister. I stopped to talk to you." Sister Joan went floorwards again.

"I don't know what you young girls are coming to," Sister Gabrielle remarked. "In my day we managed to work and to exchange the occasional scrap of conversation at the same time."

She tapped her way back down the passage. Sister Joan paused long enough to chuckle and went on with her work.

"Sister Joan, the dog got into the

parlour again." Mother Dorothy emerged from the anteroom beyond which her parlour lay, the puppy scampering round her ankles.

"I'm very sorry, Mother Dorothy." Sister Joan captured the wriggling bundle.

"I agreed to our having a dog on the premises provided the animal was trained as a guard dog and not permitted beyond the kitchen," Mother Dorothy scolded.

"Yes, of course, Mother. It's time for her training session now," Sister Joan said, escaping kitchenwards.

Alice frisked happily at the end of her lead, a mood that would rapidly change, Sister Joan knew, when she was required to walk to heel.

"Come on, sweetheart. Walkies!"

She opened the kitchen door and went out into the yard. The recent cold snap had left pools covered with a thin film of ice between the cobbles and the sky overhead was still a dull, uniform grey. From her stall Lilith, the convent pony, whickered a greeting.

"Sister Joan, put on your cloak!"

Sister Perpetua barged out of the back

door, waving the said garment ahead of her.

"Thank you, Sister." Sister Joan hung it about her shoulders.

"The idea of going out in this weather with nothing extra on! I have my hands full with the old ladies without having to break off because a silly girl catches double pneumonia!" Sister Perpetua scolded.

This was the second time in one morning that she'd been scolded like a schoolgirl, Sister Joan thought ruefully. To the older members of the community she must seem very young and inexperienced, but the plain fact was that in less than a month she would be thirty-seven years old. Not that the slightest notice would be taken of her birthday though her family would send cards. When she had taken her final vows she had left earthly anniversaries behind her. Perhaps that was one of the reasons that religious looked young. They were not obliged to count the years.

Holding the lead firmly she went through the stableyard and round the corner into the garden. This being

February Sister Martha's gardening duties were lighter and she was busily lagging pipes and checking for leaks in the cistern. Sister Joan skirted the low wall and the little cemetery beyond where one day — but not, please God, too soon — she would lie beside her sisters, and made her way along the rough sloping track that ended in a shallow flight of steps leading down to the tennis courts. Here it was safe to let Alice off the lead and begin the task of teaching her to stay and come and sit, all instructions which the puppy reacted to as if they were couched in an incomprehensible foreign tongue she had no intention of learning.

"Stay. Good girl, stay." Sister Joan backed off, Alice immediately springing after her.

"Good morning, Sister Joan. Good morning, Alice."

Sister Hilaria, emerging from the postulancy, greeted them cordially. She looked tired, Sister Joan thought, or perhaps it was the greyness of the morning.

"Are you feeling all right, Sister Hilaria?" she asked on impulse.

To enquire after the well-being of another sister could scarcely be regarded as an infringement of the rule even if it was Lent, but Sister Hilaria hesitated before she answered with some reluctance, "I'm afraid I slept badly, Sister. I was just wondering if it might be permissible for me to go over to the main house for an aspirin."

"I'll get one for you unless you think the walk would do you good," Sister Joan said promptly.

"Sister Elizabeth and Sister Marie are busy cleaning," Sister Hilaria said. "I told them — yes, I'm sure that I did tell them — that I was stepping out for a few minutes. Yes, a walk might do the trick."

"Would you like me to come with you, Sister?" Sister Joan enquired.

Sister Hilaria might well wander elsewhere, rapt in some spiritual contemplation of her own, and forget about the aspirin. There had been a time when she had marvelled at Mother Dorothy's having appointed the dreamy and absentminded nun as mistress of novices but she had begun to realize the sound sense behind the prioress's train of reasoning. Eager young postulants embarking upon the religious life needed to learn that common sense wasn't supposed to be left along with one's worldly goods at the convent door, but it was important for them to have as model a nun who was a genuine mystic even if she lacked the practical skills with which most nuns were endowed.

Sister Hilaria checked her slow stride, said in a surprised tone, "Sister Joan, Alice is with you."

"I was trying to train her to come when I called," Sister Joan said.

"Just use her name," Sister Hilaria said, raising her voice slightly as Alice went flying off into the shrubbery. "Alice, come along now."

Alice turned and trotted back to Sister Hilaria's side, treading neatly at her heels like the well-trained guard dog she was expected to become.

"Well, she won't do that for me!" Sister Joan exclaimed in exasperation.

"Probably because you don't expect her to obey," Sister Hilaria said kindly. "She is a very pretty little dog, isn't she?

But I do wish that it wasn't necessary to have a guard dog on the premises."

"In view of what happened last autumn, Sister, Detective Sergeant Mill thought it advisable," Sister Joan reminded her.

"That was a dreadful business." Sister Hilaria looked distressed. "However I doubt if anything similar will ever happen again, and a dog can only keep us from physical harm. Real evil isn't physical, is it?"

"No, Sister. No it isn't," Sister Joan said gravely.

"I was always rather struck by a remark of St Bernadette's," Sister Hilaria said, apparently flying off at a conversational tangent. "She was asked once what sanctity was and she answered that it was like perfume: only the one who was wearing it couldn't smell it."

Sister Joan who was beginning to learn how to untangle the labyrinth of Sister Hilaria's thought processes said, "And evil is a stink in the nostrils? Is that why you couldn't sleep?"

"Something is casting a shadow over us," Sister Hilaria said. Her large, pale face quivered slightly with some unexpressed emotion. "It isn't here the way I feel it. Coming like the shadow of a shadow. It troubled me. It troubled me very much, Sister."

"I'm sure nothing dreadful will happen to any of us," Sister Joan reassured.

"Not to us." Sister Hilaria gave her a faintly surprised look. "No, I have no fears for us, Sister, but the one who casts the shadow of a shadow — they stand in very great danger."

They had reached the low wall of the enclosure garden, the bare soil neatly raked, the paths still glistening with half-melted frost, the first crocuses and snowdrops rising up bravely in the borders. Perhaps it was the sudden gust of bitter wind that shook the leafless trees and set the jewelled holly bushes quivering which sent a shudder through Sister Joan which chilled her to the marrow.

"I think our little talk has done me good," Sister Hilaria said. "I hope it could not be construed as chattering during Lent, but we have been discoursing on spiritual matters, haven't we? Goodbye,

Alice. Be a good dog."

She turned and wafted back towards the tennis courts, the need for an aspirin apparently gone. People meeting Sister Hilaria for the first time were apt to glean the impression that she was slightly lacking in her wits. Those who knew her better were aware that she merely framed her thoughts on a different level.

"Is everything all right, Sister Joan?" Mother Dorothy straightened up from one of the graves she had been tidying and came over.

"Sister Hilaria marches to a different tune, doesn't she?" Sister Joan said.

"Yes, Sister. Yes she does." The prioress smiled slightly. "You haven't answered my question."

"Nothing's wrong as far as I know, Mother," Sister Joan said carefully. "Sister Hilaria came for a short walk to try to rid herself of a headache."

"She needs an assistant," Mother Dorothy said. "I told you before that when the opportunity arises I will appoint you as assistant mistress of novices, but for the moment you are more useful where you are. However whatever help you can give in any area will be appreciated."

She gave the brisk little nod that marked the end of a conversation and went off again, greyish light haloing her figure and glinting off her spectacles.

Luncheon was soup without bread. The most that could be said in its favour was that it was hot. The soup was drunk standing, each sister cupping her hands about the large earthenware mug. Afterwards the community continued with the everyday work, Mother Dorothy retiring to her parlour to wrestle with the accounts, Sister David crouched over her research work in the library above the chapel, Sister Perpetua mixing some potion in her office, Sister Gabrielle and Sister Mary Concepta propped up in the infirmary and knitting. Sister Martha led Lilith out for a demure walk and Sister Katherine retreated to her cell to work on her lace before the light began to fade.

"And you will spend the rest of your life doing the same things day after day," Jacob had said when she had told him that she was going into the convent. "Your time will be divided into little

36

parcels by the ringing of bells."

Impossible to try to explain to Jacob whose religious traditions were so different that by disciplining the physical it was easier to free the mental and spiritual. Jacob, with his keen, subtle, Semitic mind, his wild enthusiasms and prickly obstinacy placed no limits on any freedoms. Yet in the end he had found it impossible to marry a Gentile just as she had found it impossible to lay her faith aside and convert to another.

"Come on, Alice. Walkies!" she said loudly, striving to banish the ghost from the past that still occasionally obtruded itself into her thinking.

Alice who had evidently decided to understand certain words jumped up happily, and submitted to having her lead put on. Sister Joan walked round to the front of the building where green turf stretched to the walls with the great wrought-iron gates fastened back and the track that led over the moor towards Bodmin beyond.

There were no locks at the convent save those the nuns operated themselves last thing at night. There was nothing to prevent her from going beyond the gates, from taking to her heels and running free, the wind catching her short white veil and sending it flying out. She was a prisoner only of her own desire. And Jacob was long gone, probably married by now to a comfortable little wife who had given him a couple of children.

Alice was jerking at the lead, uttering short, sharp little barks of frustration.

"Five minutes then," Sister Joan said, stooping to unfasten the lead. "And straight back here again when I call you."

Alice gave her a look of dewy-eyed innocence and shot through the gates, Sister Joan sat down on a large block of stone just within the entrance, bunching her skirts beneath her in approved convent fashion, clasping her hands in her lap, one part of her mind toying with the idea of giving Alice freedom for the decade of a rosary, the other flying to the little school building where up to the previous autumn she had taught the local children too young to go to the schools in Bodmin. She had had only a handful of pupils drawn from local farmers and from the Romany camp high on the moors, but she had grown fond of them, had relished being able to slip a pair of jeans under her habit and ride Lilith to and from the solitary building. It was a great pity that the education authorities had closed it down and now bussed the children into town. Padraic Lee who supplied the convent with fish sometimes had told her on his last visit that truancy had increased.

Alice was running back before being called, barking furiously, and trying to catch her tail in her mouth as she tried to run circles on the same spot.

"Good girl!" Sister Joan captured her, clipped on the lead and straightened up to find herself looking into the deepset, burning eyes of a white-faced, grey-cloaked individual who stood, tall and solid, against the light.

Alice barked more furiously.

"Quiet girl," Sister Joan said, speaking automatically out of a suddenly dry mouth. "She — she won't hurt you — only a puppy. May I help you?" This last was purely out of mechanical politeness since the woman facing her looked as if she were capable of dealing with any situation.

"I am Sister Jerome," the other said. Her voice in contrast to her height and her strongly marked features was light and thin.

"Sister Jerome. Yes?" Sister Joan felt completely at a loss. Mother Dorothy hadn't mentioned that a visitor was expected.

"From the London house," the other said. "Lay sister."

"You mean you've come to be lay sister here?"

"This is the Order of the Daughters of Compassion?" There was deep suspicion in the tone as if Sister Jerome feared she might have landed among the Carmelites by mistake.

"Yes. Yes indeed, this — you've certainly come to the right place," Sister Joan said hastily, "but I — we were not aware that anyone had been sent."

"I understand a letter was sent from the London house."

"Then it hasn't arrived yet. Our postman doesn't come all the way up here every day. How did you get here?"

"I came on the train and got off at the station," Sister Jerome said.

"You walked here — all the way from Bodmin?"

"I am used to walking," Sister Jerome said. "I carried my overnight case and my trunk is being brought tomorrow. I trust that's satisfactory."

"Yes, of course, Sister Jerome." Sister Joan had regained some of her poise. "Do forgive me for sounding so muddled but you arrived so — so unexpectedly. I'm very happy that you're here. We've had no lay sister proper for some months and I've been filling in — I'm Sister Joan. This is Alice."

"The rule allows pets? I wasn't aware of that," Sister Jerome said.

"The rule doesn't forbid them," Sister Joan said shortly, wondering if she liked Sister Jerome very much. As a sister it was her duty to love her but liking fell into a different category. She added, "She's being trained as a guard dog. The local police thought it advisable. You may have heard of the events here last — "

"Not, I think, a subject for discussion

41

during Lent," Sister Jerome said.

"No. No, of course not," Sister Joan said. "We are not a large convent here but then our Order isn't one of the larger Orders, is it? Mother Dorothy is prioress and Sister Hilaria mistress of novices and the others you'll meet in due course. You've arrived just in time for supper and recreation."

"As lay sister I am not entitled to join in the recreation of the fully professed," Sister Jerome said repressively.

"No, but you won't be taking up your duties until tomorrow," Sister Joan said. They had reached the front doors and she was immensely relieved to see Mother Dorothy emerge, hand outstretched.

"Sister Jerome? I just received a telephone call from Mother Agnes enquiring whether or not you had arrived. Apparently a letter was sent but hasn't yet been delivered. Surely you didn't walk from the station?"

"Sister Jerome is accustomed to walking," Sister Joan said.

"Even so." Mother Dorothy ushered the newcomer within. "Come into the parlour, Sister. Sister Joan, bring us two cups, of tea, will you? Sister Jerome must be in need of one."

Sister Jerome looked as if she were in need of nothing but disappeared silently in the wake of the prioress.

Sister Teresa was chopping up cabbage when Sister Joan went into the kitchen. Sister Martha grew a great many cabbages, Sister Joan thought, and wished she would curb her enthusiasm for that particular vegetable a little.

"We have a new lay sister," she announced. "Sister Jerome has been sent from our London house."

"Weren't you there yourself, Sister?" Sister Teresa stopped chopping and looked up with interest. "Did you know her?"

"I did my novitiate there. No, she wasn't there in my time," Sister Joan said, switching on the kettle and getting out the teapot.

"What's her name?" Sister Teresa enquired.

"Sister Jerome."

"Wasn't he a rather grim kind of saint?" Sister Teresa said.

"Very grim," Sister Joan said feelingly.

43

Those entering the religious life as a Daughter of Compassion with suitable baptismal names were permitted to keep them. Others chose saints who appealed to them as models. Jerome was not among the most popular. That this sister had obviously chosen the name shed some light on her personality.

"It will be a godsend for us to have her here," she said, blotting out the uncharitable thought.

"After Easter I will be able to go into seclusion without worrying how you're going to manage," Sister Teresa said happily, continuing to chop.

The tea brewed, she poured out two cups and carried them up the passage and into the prioress's parlour. It was hard to enter what had been a grand drawing-room without the heart lifting with pleasure at the beautifully moulded cornices and ceiling, with their tracings of gold leaf, at the panels of faded exquisite silken tapestry on the walls, at the parquet floor, polished as usual to shining perfection. The overstuffed couches, the spindly-legged occasional tables, the family portraits had long since gone to be replaced by filing cabinets, a large, uncompromisingly plain desk, hard chairs and a row of wooden stools for the sisters to perch on during religious instruction, but nothing could diminish the intrinsic beauty of the apartment.

"*Dominus vobiscum.*" Mother Dorothy gave the customary salutation.

"*Et cum spiritu sancto,*" Sister Joan responded, setting down the tea, kneeling briefly. Out of the corner of her eye she could see Sister Jerome, upright as a statue, seated on the extreme edge of a chair.

"Thank you, Sister Joan." Mother Dorothy began to pour milk. "Sister Jerome will take up her duties tomorrow. Sister Teresa is due to enter seclusion after Easter so for the time being she may remain as assistant lay sister. That leaves yourself."

"Yes, Mother Dorothy?" Sister Joan tried not to look expectant.

"For the time being make yourself generally useful," Mother Dorothy said disappointingly. "Sister Jerome will occupy one of the lay cells, Sister Teresa continue to sleep in the other, so you may move

45

your things into your old cell upstairs. Thank you, Sister."

So she wasn't yet to be entrusted with the care of the novices. As she withdrew, softly closing the door behind her, Sister Joan caught and fielded a cold, burning glance from Sister Jerome's deepset eyes. It looked, she mused wryly, as if the lack of liking between them was mutual.

3

FATHER MALONE, to his great embarrassment and equally great pleasure, was being given a rousing send-off by a small but devoted band of parishioners, among whom Sister Joan stood, charged by the prioress with representing the convent. By rights the other lay sister ought to have accompanied her, but Sister Jerome was mucking out the stable and Sister Teresa not yet permitted to leave the enclosure, so with considerable relief Sister Joan had driven alone over to the station where the platform was crowded with wellwishers and passengers arriving and departing.

"Quite a turn out, Father," she commented now.

"They're very likely here to make certain they've seen the back of me for a while," Father Malone said, eyes twinkling.

"Father Stephens didn't come?"

"He had the hospital visit to make,"

Father Malone said. "I went by there last evening to say goodbye."

"*Au revoir*," Sister Joan corrected.

"Thank God, yes! For I'd not want to leave this parish now though, of course, we must go where we're sent. I've made Mother Dorothy promise that she'll write and keep me up to date with what's happening up at the convent. I've heard already that you have a new lay sister."

"Sister Jerome, yes. She seems very efficient."

"Faint praise?" He cocked a bushy eyebrow.

"I'm sure she will settle in nicely, Father."

"You know, Sister, when all the nuns in a convent are getting along splendidly I always advise bringing in a sister who's a bit of a square peg in a round hole," Father Malone said. "Does wonders for ridding a place of complacency. Now take good care of yourself, Sister Joan. Make my replacement welcome."

"He hasn't arrived yet?"

"Later today, I understand. The seminary gave him his train ticket yesterday but he has relatives in Falmouth so it's possible he stayed overnight there. He'll be along later I don't doubt. Ah! here's the train! Now where are my bags?"

He was surrounded by his congregation, borne along in the midst of them, his bags thrust after him. Someone started up a chorus of 'He's A Jolly Good Fellow'. Sister Joan moved back to the waiting-room and stood there, raising her hand in farewell as the train doors were slammed, the final goodbyes shouted through pulled down windows. They would miss Father Malone with his innocent relish for a bit of gossip, his tried and tested homespun philosophies.

The crowd was dispersing. She watched them leave, chatting, thoughts set on the day ahead. One or two acknowledged her with a greeting, recognizing her as one of the sisters from the convent, but not, she guessed, able to put a name to her. Since the school had been closed she had lost touch with many of her former pupils and their parents.

"Excuse me, Sister?"

A youngish man had emerged from the

waiting-room and was giving her a shy, questioning look.

"Sister Joan. How may I help you Father?"

Belatedly she noticed the clerical collar.

"Father Matthew Timothy," the other said.

"Father Malone's replacement? Oh, but you just missed him!" Sister Joan exclaimed.

"He left on the train. Yes, I know. I didn't wish to intrude on his leavetaking."

"He will be disappointed that he missed you," Sister Joan said.

"Oh, I doubt that, Sister," Father Timothy said deprecatingly. "He might have been so disappointed at the sight of me that he cancelled his trip!"

He smiled slightly as he spoke as if to signal that he was joking, but Sister Joan couldn't avoid the thought that his jesting concealed a very real feeling of inadequacy. Certainly there was nothing charismatic about this very ordinary man with thin sandy hair who was now lifting his suitcase up and nodding his head towards another one.

"Books, Sister. I'm afraid they're my

one extravagance. Perhaps we could get a porter."

"They're a dying breed," Sister Joan said cheerfully, picking up the extra case and finding it lighter than she had expected. "If you don't mind walking for ten minutes, Father, I'll show you the way to the presbytery."

"That's very kind of you, Sister." Father Timothy looked pleased. "You won't get into any trouble?"

"No, of course not!" Sister Joan glanced at him in surprise, then remembered that he was newly ordained and this was his first parish. Probably he was still in the state when one anxiously requests permission for everything.

"I'm afraid your Order isn't well known to me," he confessed as they left the station and began to walk along the busy street.

"We're a young Order," Sister Joan told him. "A young woman called Marie van Lowen, part Dutch, part English. She died in the gas chambers at Dachau but not before she had founded her first convents."

"But you wouldn't have met her

personally, Sister."

"I wasn't even born then," Sister Joan said with a grin. "But every postulant is told the story of Marie Lowen when she enters. We're always hopeful that the Cause for her Canonization will be introduced but these things take an awfully long time. She's not been dead for fifty years yet."

"The regulations have been tightened up considerably since Vatican Two," Father Timothy reminded her. "Before that all kinds of unsuitable candidates were being raised to the altars."

"Not so many surely, Father," Sister Joan began.

"St Christopher who is now deemed never to have existed in popular legend."

"For someone who's never existed he's protected a great many travellers!" Sister Joan said, beginning to feel irritable. The new priest, she feared, was a pedant.

"And you have a sentimental attachment to him?" Father Timothy said with a small tight smile which struck her as patronizing.

"I simply believe that when thousands of people down through the centuries have a great devotion to a particular figure then the devotion itself can bring into being a person with the attributes they admire."

"It's all in the mind, eh, Sister?" He gave her the look reserved for nuns who consider themselves to be intellectual and said immediately in a tone of relief, "Ah! I see the church just ahead of us. That will be the presbytery next to it."

"Father Stephens will probably still be at the hospital," Sister Joan said. "He went over there this morning. But Mrs Fairly will be at home, I'm sure."

"Mrs Fairly?"

"The housekeeper. She makes Father Malone and Father Stephens very comfortable." 'She nags the life out of the both of us,' Father Malone was apt to complain. "I never could understand why priests are deemed far too helpless to look after themselves when bachelors all over the country are managing to do it without any trouble."

His complaints were only halfhearted. Mrs Fairly was one of those slim, harassed-looking middle-aged widows who seem destined to spend their lives answering the door with the phrase 'I'll just see if Father's available' on their lips. Sister Joan had only met her on a couple of occasions and knew nothing of her background.

Both church and presbytery were small, walls of Cornish granite, the tower of the church square and squat. In a predominantly Protestant area the Catholics were tactful about their continuing presence though old feuds had long since died.

They walked up the short path past the variegated bulbs that were Mrs Fairly's pride and joy and Sister Joan set down the case she was carrying and rang the bell. A twitch of the muslin curtains had told her that the housekeeper had seen their arrival but considered it uncivil to be seen herself gaping out of the window.

There was a short pause and then the front door opened and Mrs Fairly, a scarf over her greying hair, a neat print overall covering her dress, appeared, a carefully judged smile of welcome on her face.

"It'll be Father Timothy? I'm delighted you got here safely, Father. Did you catch Father Malone at the station? I would have been there myself but Father Stephens went rushing out without a decent breakfast this morning so I decided to do a mixed grill. It's Sister Joan from the convent, isn't it? Did you see Father off all right?"

"And met Father Timothy at the station," Sister Joan said. "I'm afraid he missed meeting Father Malone."

"Well, Father Stephens will be along soon," Mrs Fairly said. "Come along in. You'll be wanting a cup of tea, Sister. You didn't walk down?"

"No, I drove. I should have offered you a lift, Father. I just didn't think of it."

"Please don't blame yourself, Sister." Father Timothy said, giving her a pat on the shoulder evidently of Penance intended to be consoling. "The ladies are not always expected to be practical."

"I'll show you your room, Father. Sister, will you brew the tea?" Mrs Fairly bore her charge away.

Sister Joan went through into the kitchen, vaguely aware that the housekeeper's request had been a sop to her ego after the priest's patronizing remark.

Mrs Fairly would never in a thousand years have declared herself the equal of men: had she ever thought of the matter she would probably have regarded herself as their superior.

She had just poured the boiling water into the pot when Mrs Fairly reappeared.

"I've left Father Timothy to have a wash and brush up," she said. "He's not as young as I expected. Probably had a late vocation."

"Like me," Sister Joan said.

"Well, I've always felt it was a good idea to see a bit of life first before you made up your mind about anything," Mrs Fairly said, setting out cups and saucers. "Father get off all right, did he?"

"With his fan club present," Sister Joan said with a grin.

"Well, he'll be missed," Mrs Fairly said. "Not that a holiday won't do him good. It will give Father Stephens a chance to find out how he can cope too."

It was the nearest she would allow herself to come in expressing an opinion about the handsome young curate who was, everybody agreed, all set for a bishopric one day.

"We have a new lay sister ourselves," Sister Joan said, remembering. "Sister Jerome from our London house."

"Jerome. Jerome." Mrs Fairly frowned slightly. "Now where have I? Never mind, it'll come to me, I daresay. Bring your tea into the dining-room Sister. I'll just check on the oven and add a few more mushrooms for Father Timothy and then join you."

The dining-room at the other side of the hall with the parlour leading out of it was lined with bookshelves. Glancing at the crowded, much-thumbed volumes, Sister Joan wondered where Father Timothy was going to fit in the books he'd brought with him.

"Here you are, Sister!" The object of her musings came in, looking round with the interest of a newcomer.

"There's a cup of tea for you, Father." Sister Joan handed it to him. "Do you take milk and sugar?"

"Not in Lent, Sister." The sandy brows drew together in disapproval.

"Oh. Yes, of course, Father." Sister

Joan looked rather guiltily into her own cup.

"Mrs Fairly mentioned a mixed grill." Father Timothy had lowered his voice. "Not meat during Lent?"

"It'll be grilled herrings with mushrooms, tomatoes and sauté potatoes," Sister Joan said. "Mrs Fairly knows the rules so well that Father Malone says she could probably advise His Holiness on doctrine."

The jest had made everybody smile in the convent. Father Timothy merely looked uncomfortable.

"Father Stephens will be along any time now," Mrs Fairly said, bustling in. "Shall I unpack for you, Father?"

"Thank you, but I prefer to do it myself," he said stiffly.

"I have to get back." Sister Joan put down her cup and saucer. "It was nice to meet you, Father Timothy."

"Thank you, Sister Joan. No doubt I will be visiting the convent in due course." His handshake was brief and limp.

"I'll see you out, Sister." Mrs Fairly went ahead to open the door. "You'll give my regards to Mother Dorothy? I suppose you'll be assigned other duties now the new lay sister has come?"

"Not yet," Sister Joan said. "At the moment I'm supposed to be making myself generally useful."

"Sister Jerome." Mrs Fairly screwed up her eyes and peered into the middle distance over Sister Joan's shoulder. "I'll recall where I heard that name if I don't consciously think about it. Good morning, Sister. Drive carefully."

She undoubtedly sent Father Malone off every morning with the same injunction, Sister Joan thought, as she went down the path and turned back towards the station.

In Father's case there was good reason for such a warning since the mild little man laboured under the delusion that he was an undiscovered racing driver and flung his ageing vehicle about with the beatific smile of one who believes he's an expert.

Unlocking the door of the convent car, sliding her small, trim person behind the wheel, Sister Joan hoped her own standards of driving were somewhat higher. Still it was nice to know that somebody cared. Mrs Fairly, whom she scarcely knew at all, was a pleasant woman. She wondered how she'd get on with the fresh out of the seminary Father Timothy. And how on earth would Father Timothy react to the urbane Father Stephens who wore his cassock as if it were a silk robe and filled his sermons with obscure quotations?

"It's nothing to do with me anyway," Sister Joan informed her reflection in the driving mirror, turning off on to the moorland road that wound its wide, dusty ribbon between the high banks of winter bleached heather and gorse.

She would have liked the excuse to drive over to the Romany camp and ask after her former pupils but she had no valid reason for going there, so put the desire to the back of her mind, and concentrated on the faults she'd be confessing soon at the Sacrament of Penance. After seven years as a religious the list of her faults seemed to get longer, she thought wryly. Not that there were any serious infringements of the rule to regret. Instead there were a multitude of small omissions, tiny deviations from the practice of charity and obedience, like pebbles in a wall which would be washed away from the solid base and cause the wall itself to tumble if she didn't take care.

A tall figure shambled across the track, causing her to brake sharply.

"Luther, take care!" She slowed further, putting her head out of the window to shout a warning.

The figure paused, took a few steps towards her, said in a high complaining tone, "Wasn't me did it, Sister! Wasn't me. Honest! Wasn't me!"

Sister Joan lowered her voice slightly, using the soothing accents that one needed to employ with the overgrown man whose mind sometimes worked perfectly well but at other times either flew off at a tangent or fixed itself obsessively upon some object beyond his reach. Luther had spent time in psychiatric care but now lived with his Romany relatives who had the sense to accept him as harmless if a trifle eccentric.

"I'm sure you haven't done anything,

Luther," she said. "I wouldn't worry about it if I were you."

"They'll say it was me done it," Luther persisted.

"Nobody says you've done anything wrong, Luther. You go on back home now," Sister Joan said.

"You don't come no more to the camp," he complained.

"It's Lent. Remember I told you that in Lent we don't go visiting unless it's absolutely necessary. I'll come at Easter. I promise."

"That's a while away," he said plaintively.

"It will come the way it always comes. Go home, Luther."

Leaving him to lope off, the recent anxiety already half erased from his mind by the prospect of the coloured eggs that signified Easter for him, she drove on. Luther was fine as long as he was kept occupied with small jobs around the convent grounds or was permitted to accompany his cousins when they went to sell scrap iron but when time hung heavy on his hands he was apt to start imagining things. She would ask

Sister Martha if there were any tasks he could undertake before the spring sowing proper began.

"You're late," Sister Perpetua observed when she had garaged the car and made her way to the kitchen.

"I showed Father Timothy the way to the presbytery and Mrs Fairly asked me to stay for a cup of tea. Did you want me for anything, Sister?"

"A bit of cheerful conversation if it wasn't Lent." Sister Perpetua tugged her veil into place over the two-inch span of reddish hair allowed by the rule to be revealed, and gave a rueful grin. "I don't know why but I've been at sixes and sevens this morning. Sister Gabrielle's knee is troubling her again. It must be pretty bad because she actually admitted as much and I hadn't enough of the linament left so I asked Sister Jerome to boil up some comfrey and she said she was lay sister and not infirmarian and had some penance to do anyway — left over from her last confession I suppose, since she hasn't made any confession since she got here, and Sister Teresa went off to help Sister Martha and Sister Katherine, and then Luther came bothering round — it has been a morning and a half, Sister!"

"What did Luther want?"

"Went on and on about not having done something or other. I'm afraid I was a little short with the poor creature. Temper always was my problem."

"I'm sure you had cause," Sister Joan said. "Now that I am here what do you need doing?"

"All done; I boiled up the linament myself, but it was a relief to have a bit of a grumble," Sister Perpetua said. "Did you see Father Malone off all right?"

"Me and three-quarters of his congregation," Sister Joan said.

"He's bound to have a wonderful time. What's the new priest like? Rosy-cheeked and hearty, I daresay. Priests keep getting younger."

"Early forties, I'd say. Serious; very conscious of being a religious."

"He'll get over that," Sister Perpetua said. "Don't take your cloak off. I want you to run over to the postulancy for me. Sister Hilaria was supposed to take over a tin of coffee but she left it on the table and if someone doesn't take it they won't have a decent breakfast tomorrow."

"I'll take it at once." Sister Joan picked up the tin, not bothering to comment on Sister Hilaria's absentmindedness. To do that would be like remarking that the sun rose in the east.

The novice mistress and her charges had their breakfast over in the postulancy where a small kitchen enabled them to make toast and hot drinks and helped to keep them as separate from the professed nuns as possible. Sister Jerome could easily have taken it across or boiled up the comfrey leaves. Her having to do penance sounded like a feeble excuse.

"Judge not that ye be not judged," she muttered, going out into the cold yard again.

A fine one she was to think ill of others when her own list of faults was growing longer by the minute!

Alice came bounding up from the shrubbery where she had been investigating an abandoned nest, circling Sister Joan's ankles with shrill little barks of triumph to point out she didn't have her lead on.

"Heel! Good girl," Sister Joan said hopefully, and Alice promptly bounded off again.

She'd be needing firmer handling soon if she were to earn her place as guard dog, Sister Joan thought, clutching the heavy tin and walking faster.

That was when she saw the branches half lopped through and hanging limply in the still grey air. The great oak tree which had stood for more than a century at the side of the steps leading down into the tennis court was deeply scarred, white bark showing where the outer husk of wood had been slashed and cut. Nearby a holly bush with all its branches mangled stood forlorn, its berries trembling like droplets of blood on its desecrated stems.

4

"I SUPPOSE we can take it that Luther wasn't responsible?" Mother Dorothy said.

"I'm sure he wouldn't do such a thing," Sister Joan said earnestly. "He loves being out on the moor or among the trees. And he's no history of violence."

"And there's no way of telling when it was done. After the grand silence last night and before Sister Hilaria brought the postulants across for lunch this morning."

Mother Dorothy rested her chin on her hand and frowned at the surface of her desk. Seated on the stool before her Sister Joan waited.

"Vandalism is becoming a national disease," the prioress said after a moment. "Even here there must be those who take pleasure in slashing and destroying. Such a senseless thing to do."

"Sister Hilaria says that she heard nothing unusual last night or this morning and neither did the postulants," Sister Perpetua said. "Of course with the weather being so chilly the windows were closed. I agree that it couldn't have been Luther. He'd never hurt anyone or anything."

"But someone did." Mother Dorothy frowned again. "Of course the gates are open and anyone can climb over the wall at the back. I think that we must all of us keep a sharp eye out during the next few weeks in case there is a recurrence."

"Are we going to inform the police?" Sister Perpetua Penance enquired.

"One ought to report it of course," Mother Dorothy said, "but quite honestly I fail to see what action the police could take. They are already overstretched and under-manned as it is. No, for the moment we shall merely record it and keep our eyes open. Mindless violence is always so puzzling. If a hungry person steals food one can understand the motive without, of course, condoning the action."

She raised her hand in a brief blessing. Filing out with the others Sister Joan's mind flew to the newspaper cutting up in the storeroom. She had hesitated to draw a parallel between events twenty years apart but when she had a few minutes to spare she would go up and read the item again. For the moment, however, there was the soup to be served and drunk.

In the kitchen Sister Jerome was stirring the heavy tureen, her face set in the grim lines that seemed to be habitual to it. She glanced up briefly but asked no question. Sister Joan, on impulse, said, "I'm sorry I wasn't here to help you, Sister, but someone has vandalized one of the big oaks near the old tennis courts and Mother Dorothy wished to discuss the matter with Sister Perpetua and myself. You didn't hear anything unusual late last night or this morning I suppose?"

"Nothing, Sister." Sister Jerome answered curtly, gave the soup a final stir, and waited.

"Then we'd better take lunch upstairs," Sister Joan said, a trifle put out by the other's complete lack of curiosity. "Shall I help you with the tureen?"

"I can manage." Sister Jerome grasped the handles of the large earthenware tureen, lifted it as easily as if it had been filled with feathers, and went out of the kitchen.

"Sister Samson," Sister Joan said, and surprised Sister Teresa, who was just coming in from the yard, into a giggle.

"I'm sorry, Sister. It's just that you're so amusing," Sister Teresa said hastily composing her face.

"I hope not," Sister Joan said wryly. "What a thing to be remembered for! 'She was always amusing' is hardly the kind of obituary one wishes to see read out round the other convents after one's demise."

"By then one probably wouldn't care," Sister Teresa said. "I went out to check up on Lilith."

"Oh?" Counting soup bowls Sister Joan raised a questioning eyebrow.

"Sister Gabrielle says that one of the trees has been damaged, slashed, so I went out to make sure that Lilith hadn't been injured. Some people go round slashing horses, you know."

"But that's dreadful! How do you know?"

"Sister Gabrielle mentioned it," Sister

Teresa said demurely and carried the bowls out into the passage.

Despite the lack of newspapers or television Sister Gabrielle gleaned information of events in the outer world as a bee gathers pollen. She was, thought Sister Joan, following with the napkins, a grapevine unto herself.

Standing at her place in the dining-room Sister Joan murmured her 'Amen' to the Grace and drank the soup in her bowl. Drank — spluttered slightly — and saw that the other Sisters were having equal difficulty in getting it down. Mother Dorothy was sipping hers in brief experimental bursts, Sister Perpetua openly grimacing. Only Sister Hilaria who never noticed what she ate and Sister Jerome were consuming it without any change of expression.

"Sister, Lenten fare is bleak enough already," Mother Dorothy said at last, "without your mistaking the sugar shaker for the salt cellar."

"But I — " Sister Joan bit her lip.

"I put sugar in, Mother Prioress," Sister Jerome said. "In our London house I was accustomed to flavour food with salt instead of sugar, sugar instead of salt, as a penance during Lent. I assumed it would be the same here."

"It is not," Mother Dorothy said frigidly, adding fairly, "Sister Joan, I was over-quick to accuse you of carelessness. My apologies. Perhaps you would take the time to explain to Sister Jerome that we don't add to Lenten austerities here by spoiling nourishing food whatever they may do in London."

They were filing out, returning to their duties. Sister Jerome, looking as calm as if she had just been praised instead of mildly reprimanded, was gathering up the empty bowls. Sister Jerome had also lied, Sister Joan reflected, as she hurried down to the infirmary to relieve the two old ladies of their unpalatable drink. Not in a thousand years would Mother Agnes have inflicted such a grotesque penance on her community at Lent or at any other time. Mother Agnes had been novice mistress during her own postulancy and novitiate and been elected as prioress for the customary five years just after her final profession. Tall, slim, with a Gothic profile and a voice which still bore traces of the concert singer she had once been, Mother Agnes had been a wise and shrewd prioress who disliked excess in any form.

Outside the infirmary door she paused, struck by a sudden thought. It was nearly two years since she had first come to the Cornwall house. When she had been embarking on her twelve months of seclusion Sister Jerome would have been beginning her training as a prospective lay sister. Yet she had never seen her before nor heard the name.

"Are you going to stand there all day, child?" Mother Gabrielle demanded from within, "or are you bringing some more poisonous stuff to upset our digestions?"

"I'm sorry, Sister." Sister Joan hurried into the pleasant whitewashed room where a fire burned and crocuses were spiking the bowls on the window sill. "There was a misunderstanding."

"Sugar instead of salt!" Sister Gabrielle's eagle-featured face expressed outrage.

"I'm very sorry, Sisters. Shall I make you some fresh soup?"

"Nothing at all," Sister Gabrielle said firmly. "I can't speak for Sister Mary

73

Concepta though."

"Sister?" Sister Joan glanced over at the sweet-faced old nun who sat, delicate as an ageing flower, in her wheelchair.

"Nothing, Sister. We'd not wish to be singular," Sister Mary Concepta said.

"A dictum that the new lay sister might do well to observe," Sister Gabrielle said tartly. "What is the matter with that woman? I'd call her a long-faced saint if she hasn't made it abundantly clear that she's very far from being a normally polite human being!"

"She has an unfortunate manner," Sister Mary Concepta said excusingly.

"She comes from the London house. Did you know her?" Sister Gabrielle asked.

"No, not at all. It is one of the larger convents."

"Never more than fifteen sisters in one convent," Sister Gabrielle said. "Quality is better than quantity, I suppose. What's all this about vandals getting in?"

"Some damage was done to a tree," Sister Joan said reluctantly. "It really isn't anything to worry about, Sister."

"In my mid-eighties I reserve the right

to choose what to worry about," Sister Gabrielle said. "Lads from the town I daresay. No discipline these days. What's the new priest like?"

"You can ask Father Stephens about him," Sister Joan said, catching sight of the tall, fair-haired figure through the window, "for he's on his way now. Excuse me."

She made her escape followed by Sister Gabrielle's mocking, "Lost your taste for gossip, girl? I'm astonished!"

She loved Sister Gabrielle dearly, but there were times when the latter traded on her age, and the little privileges that brought her, to be a thorn in the flesh, Sister Joan thought, hurrying through to the main hall to greet Father Stephens.

"I came round from the postulancy," he said, entering with a nod. "Mother Dorothy telephoned me to inform me of the vandalism. Very disturbing indeed, Sister."

"Yes, Father. Yes, it is." Sister Joan, relieving him of his hat, found herself suddenly liking him a little better. Disturbing, she thought, was the right word to use, and there was something very human and fallible about the pained look on his handsome young face. Usually Father Stephens knew all the answers but this event had clearly puzzled and upset him.

She led him to the antechamber, tapped on the door to signal his arrival, and then tactfully withdrew, knowing that Mother Dorothy would have informed him of the vandalism more as an act of courtesy than because she thought he might be able to help.

At least she had a few minutes to herself again. She turned towards the chapel wing, padded down the short passage that led past the two parlours with their grilled division and went into the chapel. It was tempting to stay, to kneel for a few minutes and try to regain her peace of mind but she genuflected briefly and went up the narrow stairs by the Lady Altar to the library and storerooms above.

The newspaper cutting was where she had clipped it on to the requisite pile. She drew up the hard-backed chair and sat down to study it again. The item told her no more than when she had first glanced through it however. Twenty years before when the Tarquin family still lived in the great house and no Daughters of Compassion had yet come into Cornwall a number of trees in the grounds had been badly slashed and hacked about. There was no indication in the clipping as to whether or not anyone had been found guilty of the crime. Was it a crime? She bit her lip, considering. A misdemeanour, certainly, as was damage to any property, but there was something peculiarly unpleasant about the picture rising in her mind of a shadowy figure raising an axe to strike again and again in a frenzy of destruction at a living part of nature.

Certainly there seemed nothing tangible to connect one act with the more recent vandalism. Sister Joan pushed back her chair and went down into the chapel again. It was no longer empty. Sister Jerome, arms in the cruciform position, knelt bolt upright before the altar, head flung back so that it looked almost as if she was arguing with the Divine instead of joining herself with the Sacrifice.

As she hesitated the other crossed

herself and rose in one fluid movement, turning to scour the space behind her with her deep-set eyes.

"Were you looking for me, Sister?" Her voice was dry and passionless.

"No, Sister Jerome." Sister Joan hesitated again, then said warmly, "Please don't feel badly about the sugar in the soup. You were not to know."

"I am only sorry that a little extra penance during Lent is frowned upon here," Sister Jerome said coldly.

"But Mother Agnes in the London house never encouraged excessive mortification either," Sister Joan was stung into replying, "unless, she has altered a great deal since I was there."

"I said I was accustomed to render my own food unpalatable," Sister Jerome said. "I never intimated it was general practice. However when I came here I thought the other sisters would like to share in what you are pleased to call excessive mortification."

"Only if we choose it ourselves, Sister. You were not in the London house when I was there? I don't recall — "

"There is no reason why you should,"

Sister Jerome said. "I try not to make myself conspicuous. However I may as well satisfy your curiosity by telling you that I did my initial training elsewhere and spent only eighteen months under Mother Agnes's rule. Excuse me, please."

She genuflected towards the altar and went past without any further word. Sister Joan let out her breath in a silent 'whoo'. So Sister Jerome had come from another order. Such a procedure was unusual but not entirely unknown where lay sisters were concerned. There had always been a shortage of vocations for the Marys of the enclosed and semi-enclosed orders but lay sisters, who shared few of the perquisites of the fully professed but had to exist uneasily between the cloister and the world, were like gold dust, to be cherished when they arrived. It was going to be hard to cherish Sister Jerome, she reflected, as she went back to the kitchen where a pile of potatoes waited to be peeled.

From the infirmary she could hear Father Stephens talking to Sister Gabrielle and Sister Mary Concepta. Though he lacked Father Malone's cosily confiding manner he did his best with the old ladies though he was rather too apt to go on about the twilight of one's days. As Sister Gabrielle had once tartly observed she was at the age when she didn't need reminding of it.

"Sister Joan." He was tapping on the kitchen door.

"I'm sorry, Father. I was just getting started on the vegetables. Please come in." Rinsing her hands hastily she opened the door wider.

It was so unusual for Father Stephens to honour the kitchen with a visit that she stared at him for a moment before remembering to offer him another cup of tea.

"Thank you but no, Sister. The one I had with Mother Prioress was very refreshing. You are still working as lay sister then?"

"I've been told to make myself useful wherever I can," Sister Joan said.

"No doubt until Sister Jerome settles in properly. I looked in to thank you for showing Father Timothy to the presbytery this morning. I ought to have been there myself but there was the hospital visit and we weren't sure of the exact time of his arrival," Father Stephens said.

"It was no bother," Sister Joan assured him. "Mrs Fairly was in anyway."

"Busy as ever." He sighed slightly as if the housekeeper's busyness wearied him. "Father Malone will be well on his way now. Father Timothy has requested that he be permitted to share the ministry up here at the convent. I suspect that he feels more at ease with other religious, never having had a parish before."

Sister Joan couldn't imagine Father Timothy being much at ease anywhere but reminded herself that it wasn't fair to judge on one meeting.

"Well, I must get on." Father Stephens was consulting his watch. "Thank you again, Sister. No, no, I'll see myself out. I won't interrupt your labours."

As he went out into the passage again she bit back a heartfelt wish that he would interrupt a task she had never much enjoyed. Preparing and cooking food wasn't one of her favourite occupations. For an instant her fingers ached for the feel of a brush loaded with colour, the sight of a blank canvas balanced on its easel, and then the painful craving ebbed and she picked up the potato peeler again.

The afternoon grew stormier, clouds scudding across the pale grey of the horizon. The potatoes were boiling, ready to be mashed and used to cover the boiled cabbage in a cottage pie without meat. Sister Jerome was scrubbing the back steps, careless of the cold as it pierced through habit and veil. Probably she was glad of the chance to do a bit more penance, Sister Joan thought, and ordered herself to tack on an extra decade of the rosary to remind herself to be more charitable in her thoughts.

The telephone in the passage rang, startling the silence. She hastened to answer it lest the continued noise would disturb the old ladies who were having their afternoon sleep.

"The Convent of Our Lady of Compassion. Sister Joan here."

"Sister, it's Mrs Fairly — from the presbytery." The voice was distorted by a crackling line.

"Mrs Fairly, what can I do for you?"

Sister Joan asked, crushing down a sense of impending anxiety.

The housekeeper was the last person to disturb the community with a non-urgent call.

"I'm sorry to bother you, Sister," Mrs Fairly's voice apologized, "but I wondered if you were coming down into town this week."

"I have to come in tomorrow to stock up on a few things," Sister Joan said.

"I wondered if we might have a coffee?" Mrs Fairly said.

"That's very kind of you, Mrs Fairly," Sister Joan began awkwardly, "but you know this being Lent — "

"You cut down on visits. Yes, I do know, and I wouldn't ask you but — if you could possibly meet me, Sister, I'd take your advice as to what exactly to do."

"I could call in at the presbytery," Sister Joan said.

"No. Not the presbytery. Perhaps we could have a coffee at the café opposite the chemist. Do you know it?"

"Sister Hilaria and I had a coffee there after she'd been to the dentist,"

Sister Joan said. "Mrs Fairly, is anything wrong?"

"I hope not, Sister." The voice sounded doubtful, died into a crackle and came back, blurred by atmospherics. "New lay — remembered where — not willing to trouble Father with — ten tomorrow?"

"Ten tomorrow then." Sister Joan heard the click of the receiver at the other end before she had finished speaking.

Mother Dorothy frowned slightly when her permission was sought.

"Your reason for driving into town is a purely practical one, Sister," she said reprovingly. "I do think, particularly during Lent, that social contacts should be kept to an absolute minimum."

"Mrs Fairly sounded troubled, Mother. I wouldn't have asked you otherwise."

"She has two priests living in the same house if her trouble is a spiritual one," Mother Dorothy said.

"Shall I telephone her and tell her that I can't meet her then?" Sister Joan asked meekly.

"Since you seem to have made some kind of arrangement," Mother Dorothy said, her voice edged with thick frost, "then you had better go, I suppose. Certainly it's not very sensible to start running up telephone bills. You'll tell me if the matter concerns the community, of course."

"Yes, Mother Dorothy."

"If it does not then you really ought not to concern yourself with it," Mother Dorothy was continuing. "You are scarcely qualified to offer personal advice, Sister."

"No, Mother, I'll make that clear to Mrs Fairly," Sister Joan said.

"I was going to send Sister Jerome into town with you when you next went so that you could acquaint her with the shops we patronize. Apparently she has a current driving licence and will be able to take the burden of marketing off your shoulders, but if you are requested to meet Mrs Fairly you'd better go in alone."

"I don't think," Sister Joan ventured, "that Sister Jerome would enjoy trips into town, Mother."

"Since you know nothing whatsoever about Sister Jerome's likes and dislikes," Mother Dorothy said coldly, "you really are not in a position to pass an opinion, Sister Joan."

"No, Mother."

"You had better go and check that the correct seasonings have been added to our supper," Mother Dorothy said, dismissing her.

"Yes, Mother."

Feeling less chastened than she might have done Sister Joan withdrew, distinctly cheered by the faint twinkle in her superior's eyes.

Supper was palatable despite the boiled cabbage. Whether Sister Jerome had added anything or not to her own was impossible to tell since she never altered the stony expression on her face.

"You will all have heard by now," Mother Dorothy said at the conclusion of the meal, "about the act of vandalism perpetrated in the grounds. I have, naturally, asked if any of you heard or saw anything and I've talked over the problem with Father Stephens. He agrees with me that it would be useless to inform the police. By now the culprits are probably a long way off, and even reporting it would involve our local constabulary in a great deal of unnecessary paperwork, so for the moment we will keep it to ourselves. I would ask you to be vigilant, however. If you notice any strangers in the grounds do please inform either Sister Perpetua or myself."

The community filed into recreation which, it being Lent, was more subdued than usual. Not, reflected Sister Joan, that recreation at any time was a riot of pleasure. Conversation was expected to be general with no personal details referred to and fingers were expected to keep busy with knitting or sewing.

She was tired by the time the last blessing had been given, the postulants speeded on their way with Sister Hilaria, Alice let out for the last time, the doors and the windows locked and checked, the few lights that remained burning in chapel and hall reduced to a dim red glow. The storm which had threatened seemed to have passed without breaking but the sky was a peculiar leaden shade with no trace of a moon. Perhaps it was the threat of storm that had given her this feeling of something overshadowing her, of something that hovered just out of sight.

She had moved her things back to the cell she had occupied before she became acting lay sister, leaving the two cells leading off the kitchen for Sister Jerome and Sister Teresa. The professed cells were tiny rooms opening off the narrow corridor which ran above the kitchen wing, each identical with its narrow bed, stool, hooks on the back of the door for clothes, basin and ewer. A shelf against the wall held her Missal and the book in which she noted her own spiritual progress. Since reading it made her feel somewhat miserable she seldom glanced back through the latter. The larger cell which was Mother Dorothy's domain during her term as prioress was at one side of her own, a vacant cell at the other side. On the other side of the corridor Sisters Perpetua, Katherine, David and Martha slept. The empty cell would be fitted up for Sister Teresa during her year of seclusion. Sister Joan thought of her own year of silence and of solitude, when she spoke only to her priest and mistress of novices, ate alone, wore the dense black veil that cut her off from view and curtailed her own vision of the world. Never again would Sister Teresa be so alone, yet never would she feel less abandoned, buoyed up by the prayers and gentle glances of her sisters. It was when one came into the full community, balancing spiritual with the mundane, that the real loneliness could begin. At which point in her musing Sister Joan dropped into an uneasy sleep in which she walked veiled down endless corridors, hearing somewhere a crying voice seeking help and finding none.

She was relieved when she woke before her usual time and, seeing the first streaks of dawn outside the window, was justified in rising. By the time she had cleaned her teeth, washed, and donned her habit and veil, the threatening images of the night had withdrawn and she picked up the wooden rattle and began her morning rounds with relief.

"Christ is risen!"

From one cell to the next she made the customary announcement, recalling how the loud whirring of the rattle had startled her from slumber in the early days. From each cell came the customary response, "Thanks be to God", each utterance slightly different as each member of the community struggled into awareness of anew day.

When she entered the kitchen the other two sisters were already up, and there were signs of life from the infirmary. Sister Teresa sent a cheerful morning smile. Sister Jerome kept her head lowered as she drew water for the kettles.

By 5.30 the sisters were in the chapel for the hour of private devotions which preceded early mass. Father Malone and Father Stephens drove up to the convent on a weekly rota basis to offer the mass and occasionally were a few minutes late but this morning, promptly on the half-hour, Father Timothy emerged from the tiny room that served as sacristy and began the service. There was a tiny ripple of interest among the community as he mounted the altar steps and opened the Bible.

He offered the mass with a fervour that surprised her. It was as if, outwardly passionless, he threw all the resources of his soul into the reenactment of the Sacrifice. Somehow or other she had expected something more hesitant, more pedantic.

He had obviously come in by way of the outer door and he departed the same way, not stopping to introduce himself to the community over a cup of coffee. Even Father Stephens came up to the refectory, she thought, and wondered if the new priest considered such small courtesies unnecessary.

At least it wasn't raining. She finished her early chores, took the shopping list that Sister Perpetua had written, and went out to the garage. One day they'd have to buy a new car since it was highly doubtful that this one would pass another MOT test. Settling herself behind the wheel, Sister Joan knew a short moment of regret. The old car had done good service.

It was past ten by the time she had completed her purchases, stowed them in the boot, and set off briskly for the café where Sister Hilaria had once been persuaded into a cup of coffee. At this hour and on such a cold, grey day it was almost deserted. Certainly there was no sign yet of Mrs Fairly. Sister Joan ordered tea for two and poured herself a cup, keeping an eye out through the plate glass window where the street was filling with morning shoppers. One of them, a tall, dark man with a rugged aspect, paused as he caught sight of her, hesitated, then came in.

"Good morning, Sister Joan. I thought they didn't let you out during Lent."

"Detective Sergeant Mill, how nice to see you!" She responded cordially to his firm handshake.

"Busy as ever. Are you playing truant, Sister?"

"Not guilty, Detective Sergeant Mill. I'm waiting for Mrs Fairly. She asked me to meet her here."

"When?" His glance was suddenly keen.

"At ten this morning but she's a little late — oh, she telephoned the convent yesterday afternoon. Why?"

"May I join you, Sister?" He sat down and reached for the extra cup. "Was Mrs Fairly a particular friend of yours?"

"We don't have particular — you said

92

'was'. Has something happened?"

"I'm afraid I've just come from the presbytery," he said, pouring tea carefully. "Mrs Fairly was found this morning by Father Stephens. Suicide, I'm afraid. No doubt about it at all."

5

"**D**EAD?" Sister Joan's hand rose automatically to bless herself as she uttered the word.

"I'm afraid so, Sister. We were called in at seven this morning."

"Not the medical authorities?" She sipped her tea trying to take in what had happened along with the soothingly hot liquid.

"Father Stephens rang the station. He had dialled 999 and when the operator asked if he wanted Fire, Police or Ambulance he blurted out the latter two. I was on early call so I went along to the presbytery."

"And she was dead?"

"Had been for several hours according to the doctor. Apparently she gets up around five-thirty every morning and gets everything ready for Father Malone and Father Stephens."

"One of them comes up to the convent to offer mass at six-thirty in our chapel while the other offers a later mass at seven-fifteen in the parish church," Sister Joan nodded. "The new priest, Father Timothy, was at the convent this morning."

"Father Stephens became anxious when six o'clock came and there was no sign of Mrs Fairly but he left it a further half-hour before he tried to rouse her. By then Father Timothy had already left for the convent. Father Stephens rang at once and we got there a couple of minutes ahead of the ambulance."

"You said — suicide?" Sister Joan set down her cup and pressed her hands together tightly.

"There was an empty bottle of Valium," Detective Sergeant Mill said. "It was on her bedside table. Apparently she was prescribed the drug about six years ago after her husband died to help her through the trauma. She went on taking it — no more than a couple of tablets a day but even that amount can become addictive."

"Then it could have been an accident," Sister Joan said eagerly. "It's possible that continual use of a drug can cause it to pile up in the system, perhaps?"

"Not Valium," he said. "Anyway she'd had her prescription renewed only a couple of days ago. There were forty tablets in the bottle. Father Stephens recalled her taking it out of her shopping bag when she brought in some groceries. She'd evidently crushed the lot into a paste and drunk them with tea and a splash of whisky."

"How do you know that?"

"She was in the habit of adding a splash of whisky to her last cup of tea at night. She used to brew it in the kitchen and take it up to drink when she was in bed."

"Whisky and Valium aren't very safe partners."

"She took two mild-strength tablets in the mornings and she had her tipple last thing at night by which time the drug would have passed through her system anyway. No, there were traces of the powdered tablets in the dregs of the tea and whisky. Nobody could have drunk that by accident."

"There wasn't any note?"

"Nothing at all. People don't always

leave notes behind, you know. Father Stephens said that she'd seemed *distraite* last evening. He got the impression that there was something she wanted to say to him but he was busy all evening telling the new priest about his parish duties so the opportunity didn't arise."

"She wanted to speak to me," Sister Joan said. "She rang the convent and asked me if I was coming into town for any groceries this morning and, if so, would I meet her here for a chat."

"She didn't mention what it was she wished to talk about?"

"Something she'd remembered — " Sister Joan hesitated. "Then the line started to crackle and she rang off. I asked Mother Dorothy for leave to meet her here and came along this morning."

"You said that you don't have particular friends," Detective Sergeant Mill said, "but you know as well as I do that even nuns like some people more than others."

"I hardly knew Mrs Fairly at all," Sister Joan said. "Yesterday, after Father Malone's send-off, I showed Father Timothy to the presbytery and she asked me in for a cup of tea before I went back to the convent. She seemed a nice, ordinary woman, rather proud of being housekeeper for the priests — not in a nasty way but being in that job does confer a certain status in the parish."

"Was she upset about Father Malone going away for a year?"

"Well, naturally she was going to miss him — oh no!" Sister Joan broke off, her dark-blue eyes twinkling despite her distress at the news she had just heard. "If you're thinking she had a crush on Father Malone, forget it. Contrary to popular myth housekeepers don't fall in love with their priests, and Father Malone is scarcely likely to inspire an unrequited passion. No, she was sure that she was going to miss him but she was looking forward to having a newcomer to do things for and boss about. Fuss over, I ought to say. In a maternal sort of way. Certainly she wasn't in any deep depression when I saw her yesterday."

"But she was — *distraite* when she spoke to you over the telephone?"

"It was merely an impression I had. She sounded — uncertain, puzzled about something or other. Anyway we agreed to meet and then I had to go and ask for leave from Mother Dorothy."

"Make your arrangements and then ask for permission?" His voice teased her.

"It was an oversight," she said, her mouth quirking. "Anyway Mother Dorothy decided it was better to allow me to have my meeting rather than waste money on a phone call cancelling it, and there was always the possibility that I might have been able to help out in some way."

"Don't blame yourself in this affair," he said quickly. "It isn't your fault that she decided to put an end to herself."

"She couldn't have committed suicide," Sister Joan said flatly. "I'm sorry — but I cannot possibly believe that for one moment."

"Because she was a Catholic? Sister, Catholics do sometimes commit suicide."

"Not Mrs Fairly." She spoke flatly and with conviction. "She wasn't the type."

"How many suicides have you known personally, Sister?"

"None really. That makes no difference. Mrs Fairly didn't commit suicide. She

99

may have taken mild doses of Valium and she was certainly troubled about something but she wanted to talk about it with me. And she was fond of Father Malone; she'd not have been so selfish as to kill herself the instant his back was turned."

"Then you're saying she was murdered?"

He spoke mildly enough but the word made an ugly pattern in the air.

"No, of course not! That's completely ridiculous!" she said sharply.

"As you say." He finished his tea and rose, bringing out a handful of change.

"I was the one ordered the tea," she began.

"And I helped you to drink it. I'll put it on the expense account. How are they up at the convent?"

"Very well, thank you. We have a new lay sister. Sister Jerome."

"And what job are you doing at the moment?"

"General dogsbody," she said lightly. "I help out where I'm needed."

"I'm almost sorry that I won't be needing your help in this affair," he said.

"You make it sound as if I was permanently attached to the local police force."

"Not at all," he said easily. "You're a religious with no criminal expertise at all, but when there's something to be discovered you do seem to be in the right place at the right time."

"Mother Dorothy would call it the wrong place at the wrong time."

"And what would you call it?" he challenged.

"An interruption to my spiritual progress," she said firmly.

And excitement to lift her spirits when the day-to-day routine became too tedious to endure. The incisive conversation of a man instead of the bland chatter of the daily recreation. The opportunity to re-enter, however obliquely, the world she had renounced.

"It was nice seeing you again," she said, denying the thoughts bubbling up in her. "I'm very sorry to learn about Mrs Fairly. I will tell Mother Dorothy though I expect Father Stephens will have already telephoned her. Do you know if she had any family?"

"A niece. Father Stephens said he would inform her of her aunt's death. The body has been taken to the mortuary by the way."

"For an autopsy? Then you do think — ?"

"As a matter of routine. Attempts were made to revive her in the ambulance but she'd been dead for several hours. It was straightforward suicide, Sister. The inquest will be a routine matter. 'Suicide while the balance of the mind was disturbed' probably."

"Very neat and tidy," Sister Joan said. "Thank you for the tea, Sergeant." She went out ahead of him, turning briefly to smile before she walked swiftly back to her car.

Detective Sergeant Mill was an irritant in her existence. She liked him, respected his professionalism, had helped him out more than once, but the rigid line she drew between them, though of her own making, only served to remind her that she was not free to respond to any overture of affection no matter how innocent. He had mentioned once that he had two boys and that his marriage was unhappy but she hadn't invited any further confidences and he had offered none. She hoped he had sorted out his marital difficulties but knew she would never enquire.

Driving back across the moor, automatically changing gears, swerving to avoid a reckless young rabbit, she found her thoughts occupied with Mrs Fairly. Twenty-four hours before the housekeeper had been a living, breathing, human being and now she was bone and flesh laid on a mortuary slab, the tag of 'Suicide' already being applied to her. A middle-aged, respectable, Catholic woman whose small faults had been as nothing set against the wickedness of the world had suddenly and unaccountably become agitated and depressed and killed herself with a huge overdose of Valium crushed into a paste and mixed with tea and whisky. Such things did sometimes happen. But not this time. Not this time! Her every instinct told her that this suicide was too neat, too — convenient for somebody? What was it that Mrs Fairly had said exactly over that crackling telephone line? Something about the new lay — ? New lay sister? Sister Jerome? She banged her fist on the rim of the driving wheel as the words that Mrs Fairly had used, not over the telephone, but as she was seeing her out of the presbytery returned to her. Mrs Fairly said she'd read about Sister Jerome somewhere, but couldn't recall exactly where. If she didn't think too hard about it the answer would come to her. And then it had apparently come and she'd wanted to discuss the matter with someone.

"Only she didn't get the chance," Sister Joan said aloud.

And she wasn't going to get the chance to pursue the subject. There were no suspicious circumstances accompanying the death, no chance of it having been an accident, no way she could think of in which a healthy, vigorous woman could have been forced to swallow such a concoction.

An unwelcome thought struck her as she drove through the gates. Was it possible that she craved the excitement of a possible murder? The notion was disquieting in the extreme since it clashed with all her longings for a peaceful, uncluttered life.

"Your first loyalty must be to God, the second to the rule of our Order, the third to the rest of your community, the rest to those, whether lay or religious, who seek your help or would profit from your prayers."

She could hear the beautifully modulated tones of Mother Agnes, visualize her former superior's grave, Gothic features. That had been when she herself had been a postulant and what one learned as a postulant formed the kernel of the whole fruit of one's future religious life. Edging the car round into the garage Sister Joan wished she had a simpler, less cluttered personality. For the other sisters priorities seemed clear. For herself there was always the inner conflict.

"You were a very long time, Sister," Mother Dorothy said, coming out of the back door as Sister Joan lugged in the groceries.

"I'm sorry, Mother. I waited for Mrs Fairly but Detective Sergeant Mill was passing by the café and came in to tell me what had happened."

"Father Stephens was good enough to telephone me about twenty minutes ago," Mother Dorothy said. Behind her gold-coloured spectacles her eyes were troubled. "I only knew Mrs Fairly very slightly but the news shocked me greatly. Do you think her request for a meeting with you this morning was linked with whatever was preying on her mind?"

"I've no idea, Mother. It's possible, but she didn't seem to me to have something so serious on her mind that it would lead her to do such a thing."

"Let me help you with the bags, Sister." The prioress relieved her of a large one and looked at it critically. "Plastic has its detractors, I understand," she said, "but these make excellent growbags for Sister Martha's vegetables and fruit bushes. Let Sister Jerome put the groceries away and come through to the parlour."

Sister Jerome who was on her knees, cleaning the oven as vigorously as if she were punishing it, rose silently and took the bags, lifting them without apparent effort on to the kitchen table. Sister Joan lingered to take off her cloak and her overshoes before following the prioress.

"Sit down, Sister." Mother Dorothy indicated a stool and herself took the high-backed chair reserved for the prioress. She had held the post now for nearly two years and in three more would be replaced by whichever one of her sisters was voted for by the others.

"Since you have already learned from Detective Sergeant Mill of the recent sad and shocking event there is no need for me to discuss the details with you," Mother Dorothy was continuing. "I'm sure if you had any information bearing on the matter you would have passed it on to Detective Sergeant Mill. I shall merely inform the rest of the community that Mrs Fairly, whom few of them even knew by sight, has died suddenly and we will, of course, offer the customary prayers. I must say that I was exceedingly shocked when Father Stephens told me what had happened. I feel particularly sorry for Father Malone."

"Is he to be told?" Sister Joan looked up sharply.

"Father Stephens feels and I agree with him that it would serve no good purpose to spoil Father's pleasure in his trip by telling him yet especially as there is nothing he can do that cannot be done equally well by others. In a month or two, by which time he may well have begun to wonder why he hasn't heard anything from Mrs Fairly, Father Stephens will write and tell him what has occurred. If it were a death as the result of a sudden illness, an accident even, then one might not mind for him so much, but he will blame himself for not having realized the poor woman was so near desperation. It must have been a brainstorm surely."

"I don't think Mrs Fairly did kill herself," Sister Joan said.

There was a little silence. Mother Dorothy took off her spectacles, wiped them carefully, replaced them on her snub nose, and folded her hands on the flat-topped desk before her.

"I assume you have a good reason for asserting that?" she said.

"Not really, Mother." Sister Joan flushed slightly. "I hadn't exchanged more than a brief greeting with Mrs Fairly until yesterday morning and even then we only had a few words. She gave me a cup of tea while she was putting on some extra breakfast for Father Timothy, but she was so — so ordinary, and stolid, and cheerful. Even when she rang me up she didn't sound in the least desperate, merely a little puzzled and perturbed — "

"About what?"

Sister Joan's rosy cheeks grew rosier. To have told Mother Dorothy that Mrs Fairly believed she knew where she had seen Sister Jerome's name before would be to focus attention on the newcomer which might be quite unjustified since what Mrs Fairly had remembered might have no bearing on her death.

"She wasn't very clear," she said at last, substituting the essence of truth for its literal meaning. "The line was crackling and so I said I would meet her if possible and she rang off."

"What makes you so certain that she didn't take the drug overdose deliberately then?" Mother Dorothy asked.

"I don't know, Mother." Sister Joan spread her hands helplessly. "I suppose that, like you, I find it painful to contemplate that someone could reach such a pitch of despair that they would throw away the life God gave them, but there's something else. Mrs Fairly was a splendidly caring housekeeper — Father Malone used to joke that she fussed over him and Father Stephens too much, but he did appreciate her good qualities and — well, I just can't believe that she would wait until Father Malone had just embarked upon a wonderful series of pilgrimages, and then run the risk of spoiling it all for him by killing herself. She wasn't so selfish!"

"Did you say this to Detective Sergeant Mill?"

"Not really. I hadn't thought it out properly then. I did say that I couldn't believe that Mrs Fairly had killed herself but he said that there was no possibility of it having been an accident and no evidence that it had been anything else, so the inquest will be a virtual formality.

Mother Dorothy was frowning, not in displeasure but with a concentrated ferocity that intimated equally concentrated thought.

"Father Stephens made a request of

me," she said at last. "Until a new housekeeper can be appointed both he and Father Timothy will require someone to cook and clean for them. He wanted to know if I could spare one of the sisters for a week or so. I told him that I would consider the request and let him know my answer as soon as possible. It seems to me that it might be a good idea to send you down to the presbytery as temporary housekeeper. Mind, I don't order you to go. To have to leave the enclosure overnight especially during Lent is a great sacrifice, but this is the season of penance, so you may care to think about it. If by your going you could find out that poor Mrs Fairly died accidentally and not by her own hand then it would lift a great burden from Father Malone when the time comes for him to be told."

Sister Joan was silent. Her first impulse had been to declare that she would gladly go down to the presbytery if there was the smallest chance of her uncovering the truth, but her immediate reaction following that impulse had been a terrible doubt that the search for the truth might be too closely bound with her own human curiosity, her own longing to continue to play some part in the world she had renounced.

"It would entail your having to walk down into town," Mother Dorothy said, "since the car may well be needed here and Lilith would have no proper stabling in town. At the least you will be smoothing the running of the household during the funeral, the arrival of any relatives and so on. I am not sending you to poke and pry, Sister, but should something come to your attention then you must of course bring it to the attention of the proper authorities. But the decision must be yours, Sister."

"I shall go then," Sister Joan said, "but to be absolutely honest with you, Mother, I'm not sure of my own motives in doing this."

"All our motives are usually a trifle muddled," the prioress said. "I'll ring up Father Stephens at once and tell him you are on your way. You may telephone me if you get into any difficulties and you will, of course, try to follow the routine of the enclosure as far as is commensurate with your duties as housekeeper. I will impress on Father Stephens that every effort must be made to engage a full-time housekeeper as quickly as possible. That will be all, Sister. Go and pack a bag with whatever you might require for a week's stay. You had better take some money too for any expenses you might incur. Two pounds should be more than sufficient. Don't waste it."

Kneeling for the blessing Sister Joan maintained her grave expression. It would be difficult to squander two pounds in the direction of riotous living, she mused, and felt her amusement drain away as she closed the door behind her and faced the fact that, without actually saying so, Mother Dorothy had sent her out on a mission of detection.

6

SHE was near the little schoolhouse on the moor when Father Stephens drove towards her, slowing and stopping as he leaned out to say, "Sister Joan, I am on my way to give you a lift to the presbytery. Put your bag into the back and I'll turn about."

"This is very kind of you, Father." She slung her bag into the back and climbed into the passenger seat. "I expected to walk into town."

"So Mother Prioress told me but since we are to be provided with a temporary housekeeper the least I can do is bring her into town." He was turning the car, nodding towards the schoolhouse as he remarked, "It seems a pity that it should be closed."

"It's bureaucratic nonsense," Sister Joan said. "The school served a real need in the local community but nobody cares about that any more. We all have to fit into neat official slots these days."

"But at least it gives you the opportunity to spend more of your time in the enclosure. Your leaving it in order to help us out is appreciated, Sister. Mother Dorothy told me that she had left the decision to you and that you agreed without hesitation. That must be a considerable penance."

"When you've tasted my cooking, Father," Sister Joan said wryly "you might start wondering who is doing penance."

"I'm sure you're too modest about your accomplishments, Sister." He showed his excellent teeth in a dry little smile. "Father Malone and I have been somewhat spoilt up until now, I fear. Among her other virtues Mrs Fairly numbered great culinary skills."

"Her death must have been a very great shock to you, Father," Sister Joan said.

"Very great, Sister. Indeed I am still feeling somewhat numb," he confessed. "I dread having to inform Father Malone eventually but until after the inquest there is no point in spoiling his pilgrimage. I am only thankful that his financial situation

115

doesn't permit him to make long-distance calls to the presbytery."

"She's been with you for six years?"

"Since her husband died. Of course Father Malone was coping by himself at that time. By the time I arrived she was well established. A very discreet and hardworking woman. Most reliable in the carrying out of her duties."

He was turning into the high street. Another few minutes would bring them to the presbytery. Sister Joan said quickly, "A sad beginning for Father Timothy."

"Difficult certainly, though as they had only just met her death has not affected him in a personal way. He was actually offering holy mass at your chapel when I found her. I had left her as long as possible but since, in my memory, she had never overslept I eventually went upstairs, knocked and called, and then opened her bedroom door. I fancied at first she had suffered a heart attack. Her face was contorted. Then I saw the empty bottle, the dregs of the previous night's drink."

"Contorted? I thought she had taken Valium."

"Ah, you imagined as I did that dying of a drug overdose is like going to sleep," Father Stephens said. "Apparently not. As brain damage occurs there are often severe convulsions apparently. The doctor explained it to me."

"And there was no note?"

"Note? Ah, suicide note. No nothing at all. That must surely prove that she had some kind of brainstorm. When the mind is disturbed the sin of self-slaughter is no longer a sin. I am confident that is the verdict which will be returned. Come along, Sister, and I'll show you your room."

It was, she reminded herself, only a room even if less than twenty-four hours before someone had died in it. Father Stephens, murmuring something about taking her time as they were managing with sandwiches for lunch, withdrew tactfully, leaving her to stare round a fair-sized apartment with a distressingly varied pattern of roses and buttercups on the wallpaper, faded curtains partly drawn, and a narrow bed that had been stripped and the mattress turned.

Mrs Fairly's clothes hung in the

wardrobe and were folded neatly in the drawers of the dressing-table. On the top of the dressing-table were two photographs in silver frames and a modest plastic-backed hairbrush next to a box of face powder and a much worn pink lipstick, evidence that the housekeeper had had her harmless little vanities.

Apart from the bed, wardrobe and dressing-table the room contained a chair, a small bedside table with a radio alarm clock on it, and a copy of a Mills and Boon romance with a pair of reading spectacles laid on top. There was already a faint smear of dust on the spectacles which Mrs Fairly, judging from the shining surfaces elsewhere, would never have tolerated.

There was a tap on the door and Father Stephens's voice sounded again from the landing.

"There is a large suitcase under the bed, Sister. Mrs Fairly used it when she took her week's holiday in August. Perhaps her things could be put in it, ready for her niece when she comes?"

"I'll see to it, Father." Sister Joan bent and pulled out the suitcase.

Slightly to her disappointment it was empty save for two holdalls folded away under the expanding lid. She opened the wardrobe and began to take out the few garments hanging there, a winter coat with a fake fur trim on the collar, a light edge-to-edge jacket with a pleated skirt, two pairs of sensible low-heeled shoes, a pair of sandals, a tweed suit, three print dresses in varying thicknesses and identical styles. Conquering her feeling that she was picking over dead bones she felt the pockets but they were empty. In her personal habits Mrs Fairly had been neat as a regiment. The top shelf of the wardrobe yielded a straw hat and two felt berets with ornamental pins skewering them.

The dressing-table drawers held neatly folded underwear in pink nylon and blue cotton, a box of handkerchiefs, a smaller box containing a few modest pieces of costume jewellery, a phial of eau de cologne, and a packet of letters secured by an elastic band. She flicked through them swiftly but they were all from someone called Sylvie who headed them to 'Dear Auntie Anne'. Obviously

Mrs Fairly had been fond of her niece and perhaps a little lonely too since she had kept all the letters so meticulously. Of the housekeeper's life before she had come to work as housekeeper at the presbytery there were no signs at all.

Apart from the two photographs on the dressing-table: Sister Joan picked them up in turn and studied them. A much younger Mrs Fairly, in a long white dress with a spray of carnations, smiled out of the frame next to a young man who looked as if he wasn't wearing very comfortable shoes. He looked to the last degree completely ordinary and unexciting, yet this was the husband whose death had caused his widow to resort to Valium to combat her nerves. Reminding herself that not all men who inspired such devotion were Hollywood handsome she took up the second photograph and looked at the smiling face of a schoolgirl. Across the corner in a round hand was scrawled, 'To Auntie Anne and Uncle Ben, with love for Christmas'. The girl then must be a younger Sylvie. Probably they had made a particular favourite of her because their own union was childless.

There was a sadness about all of it but nothing that could give any clue to the reason for Mrs Fairly's having swallowed sufficient Valium to kill her. She put the photographs on top of the suitcase, snapped it shut and pushed it under the bed again.

Her own things took scarcely a fraction of the available space. Having hung up her dressing-gown, put her clean underwear in the dressing-table drawer and her toilet bag and towel on top, she opened the door and went along the corridor to locate the linen cupboard where she assumed there would be clean bedding. It was there, as neat and pristine as everything else. Taking sheets and a blanket back into the bedroom she wondered if she could even begin to live up to Mrs Fairly's standard of housekeeping, and seriously doubted it.

"Are you coming down for lunch, Sister?" Father Stephens called up from the hall. Sister Joan left the bedmaking and went downstairs. In the dining-room a plate of fish-paste sandwiches and a large jug of coffee waited. She smelled the aroma of the coffee with pleasure, noticed that the sandwiches looked fresh and appetising, and said regretfully, "During Lent we have only soup for lunch, Father. Perhaps I could open a tin?"

"My apologies, Sister, but I completely forgot. Yes, please do. The kitchen is your domain now. You don't mind if I — " He looked at the sandwiches.

"You go ahead and eat, Father," she assured him. "I'll go and explore the kitchen cupboards and try to work out some menu for tonight."

"Mrs Fairly always goes — used to go — shopping today for all the dairy foods," he said. "She didn't buy in bulk."

The kitchen was a larger room than the dining-room, with a rocking chair near the window and a view of the back garden. A small television set in the corner and some magazines on the shelf next to some knitting told her that the housekeeper had been in the habit of sitting here in the evenings. The cupboards held tinned food but only the remains of a loaf and half a pint of milk. If Mrs Fairly had killed herself she had chosen a most inconvenient day on which to do it, Sister Joan reflected, as she opened up a tin of tomato soup and heated it.

The soup was more acidic than the fresh soup that the community enjoyed but she drank it down, turned her gaze resolutely from the hunk of bread, and sat down to make a shopping list.

There were voices from the dining-room. Father Timothy had evidently come in. After a few moments his spare figure loomed in the doorway.

"Good afternoon, Sister Joan. This is a sad occasion which brings you here," he said.

"Yes, Father, very sad." She rose politely. "I am just making out a shopping list. Will fish and peas and mashed potatoes suit you and Father Stephens this evening?"

"I am surprised that you allow such mundane considerations as food to occupy your mind at such a time," he said stiffly. "For my own part I shall eat only the vegetables. This is Lent, you know, Sister."

"Yes, Father Timothy. I did know." She answered shortly, resisting the impulse to scowl at him.

"And we ought to be considering what we can give up in order to lift the displeasure of the Lord."

"Is the Lord displeased?" she enquired in surprise.

"There has been a suicide here, Sister." His voice was heavy with reproach. "You cannot expect the Lord to be pleased with this household."

"Surely we're each of us responsible for our own actions, Father. Sin is a very personal thing and we don't know yet what caused Mrs Fairly's death."

"You have a liking for theological argument, Sister." He made it sound as if he were accusing her of a liking for sniffing cocaine.

"Not really, Father, but I do have opinions of my own," she said coldly. "If you will excuse me I have to get to the shops."

"Certainly, Sister. Benediction is at six-thirty so Father Stephens tells me."

"I'll be there," she said shortly, and went back to her shopping list, deciding that if Father Timothy was so keen on boiled vegetables she'd make him a panful of cabbage, and feel guilty about it later.

Outside the gate a few people were hanging about, staring at the presbytery. News of the death had attracted the usual morbid sightseers. Sister Joan closed the gate with a decided little click and walked briskly towards the shops.

"Out gadding again, Sister Joan?"

Detective Sergeant Mill was crossing the road towards her.

"Shopping for the presbytery." She choked back a laugh. "Nothing so frivolous as gadding, I'm afraid."

"You're at the presbytery?"

"As temporary housekeeper until a permanent one is appointed. I have permission."

"Have you time for a cup of coffee?" he asked.

"No — yes. Yes I have, if it's important."

"Ten minutes of your time no more. And, yes, it is important. Where's your shopping list?"

"Here, but why?"

"Constable Petrie hasn't anything particular to do. I assume the items are all charged up? Wait in the café."

Sister Joan meekly relinquished her basket and shopping list and watched him go across the road to where the young constable he'd been talking to still stood. If Constable Petrie resented being turned into an errand boy he gave no sign of it, saluting smartly before he went off with basket and list. She walked the few yards to the café, reminding herself that this was not a social occasion. Detective Sergeant Mill clearly wanted to discuss something of importance.

"Two coffees, please." Joining her, he slid long legs under the table and beckoned the waitress. "Would you like some cake, Sister?"

"I'd love some but it's Lent. You have some though."

"I had a late lunch. Been up at the hospital."

"Oh?" Pouring the coffee she glanced up at him with interest.

"Just to check up." He was frowning slightly. "There was no reason not to think Mrs Fairly died by her own hand

126

but you seemed to have an instinct that she wouldn't have done such a thing and I respect your intuition, Sister. Not just yours either. The best officers are those who not only check all the facts, follow up all the leads, but use their own intuition as well. Anyway I asked the doctor to take a much closer look at the body which he did."

"And?" Forgetting the coffee she stared at him.

"Not a lot," he admitted. "But there was a needle puncture on the inside of her wrist. I assume she wasn't a junkie?"

"I'm positive she wasn't. Valium would have been the strongest thing she ever took."

"Well, the puncture's there. No blame to anyone for not having seen it sooner. There was no reason to look for anything unusual. Anyway he agreed to do some further tests. Nothing official as yet but merely to make that final check over. I thought you might like to know."

"Yes. Yes I would. You'll want me to keep it to myself?"

"Strictly. I wasn't going to say anything

until we had a result one way or the other but when I saw you just now the meeting seemed fortuitous. Are you sleeping at the presbytery or coming in every day?"

"Sleeping there just for a week." She sipped her coffee, adding, "In Mrs Fairly's room."

"They didn't give you another one?"

"There are only four bedrooms, one for each of the priests, one for visiting clergy, and the housekeeper's room."

"Which by now will have been tidied up and polished, I suppose?"

"It was very clean to begin with. I have packed away Mrs Fairly's clothes ready for her niece to have when she arrives."

"Did you glean any information about her — the housekeeper, I mean? The kind of woman she was?"

"I didn't pry," she said with dignity. "There was nothing to pry into anyway. Very few personal effects at all, just a couple of photographs of her own wedding and one of her niece as a schoolgirl and a bundle of letters from her niece. Clothes, some inexpensive jewellery, powder, lipstick — nothing.

There wasn't any reason for anyone to kill her."

"Well, perhaps nobody did," he said. "You haven't any idea why she wanted to talk to you?"

Sister Joan hesitated, her cheeks reddening. She had a fairly shrewd idea that Mrs Fairly had remembered about Sister Jerome but since Sister Jerome had been tucked up in bed in the convent at the time that Mrs Fairly died she couldn't possibly have been involved.

"I can't say that I have," she said at last.

"Hmm." He shot her a keen look but didn't pursue the subject, merely remarking as they finished their coffee, "Well, if anything pertinent to what is still a very unofficial enquiry were to come up I know you'd do the right thing. I can't say that I'm very happy to think of you staying at the presbytery."

"I honestly don't think that there's a maniac going round killing housekeepers," Sister Joan said.

"Almost certainly not, but keep an eye open anyway. I'd better get back to the station. Here comes Constable Petrie with the groceries."

"I paid for them myself, Sister." Constable Petrie said, entering the café, put down the laden basket and a bulging carrier bag with relief.

"I'll see you're reimbursed, Constable. Father Stephens didn't give me any money before I came out so I assumed they'd be charged but perhaps she did pay cash. I'll ask him about it."

"Don't worry about it, Sister. You need a hand to carry this lot?" Constable Petrie enquired.

"No, I can manage fine. Thank you again." She spoke absently, a slight frown between her brows.

"Something wrong, Sister?" Detective Sergeant Mill was looking at her.

"Nothing in particular," she said. "Thank you for the coffee and thank you for doing the shopping, Constable Petrie. It was most obliging."

It was probably nothing at all, she told herself, as she lugged the groceries back to the presbytery, but there had been no handbag among Mrs Fairly's effects. Its absence hadn't occurred to her since it was years since she herself had had any occasion to carry a handbag, but the remarks about payment had struck a chord. Every laywoman she had ever known had owned a handbag, receptacle for keys, purse, tissues, library tickets, bills to be paid, old bus tickets — there had been no handbag in the bedroom. Neither had she noticed one in the kitchen. And would Mrs Fairly have left it in the kitchen anyway? Sister Joan guessed that she would have been more likely to take it upstairs last thing at night along with her hot tea into which she would pour her nightly tipple of whisky.

"You were a long time, Sister." Father Timothy opened the front door as she came up the path.

"There was a lot to buy," she said shortly. "Is Father Stephens here?"

"In the study, writing his sermon for high mass on Easterday."

"So soon?" Sister Joan reflected for a moment and then nodded. Father Stephens took a certain literary pride in his sermons. They contained much that was erudite and philosophical. No doubt he worked on them for a long time, assiduously polishing each mellifluous phrase, unlike Father Malone who frequently forgot to write anything at all but still managed to speak fluently for the allotted fifteen minutes.

While she was preparing the evening meal she took time to look round the kitchen, to open a cupboard here, a drawer there. No handbag was revealed. It had to be somewhere, she reasoned. Handbags didn't just get up and walk away.

The evening paper plopped through the letter box. Picking it up and smoothing it out her eye caught the black headline: *Mutilated Body Found On Railway Line*.

"Is that the paper, Sister?" Father Stephens had emerged from the little room dignified by the name of 'study' at the back of the hall.

"It's here, Father."

Handing it to him she saw the look of faint distaste on his face as he looked down at it.

"Good news doesn't make headlines, I suppose," he said.

"I'm afraid it doesn't, Father," Sister Joan said.

"I have been working on my Easter sermon. Father Malone generally gives it but as he's not here the task will fall to me. Unfortunately I cannot bring any sense of joy into my thoughts at the moment."

"Do you know when Mrs Fairly's niece is due?" she asked.

"She is coming down tomorrow, I understand. I spoke to her very briefly on the telephone. Mrs Fairly had given the name and address to Father Malone as her next of kin when she first came here otherwise I'd have been puzzled as to whom to inform."

"Wouldn't Mrs Fairly have had the address in her address book anyway?"

"I really couldn't say." He looked at her blankly. "I don't recall Mrs Fairly ever writing many letters except to her niece. When Miss Potter arrives — her name is Sylvia Potter — we can arrange the funeral details. Was there anything else you wanted, Sister?"

"I shall need a key, Father, so I can come in and out without disturbing you."

"A key. Of course. Mrs Fairly had

one — two, for the back and front doors. She kept them on a small hook in the kitchen, I think."

"Not in her handbag?"

"I suppose she put them into her handbag as she went out. I really can't say, Sister. I'll glance through this and then prepare for benediction. I have decided to say nothing about the recent sad affair. No point in fuelling the flames of scandal."

He turned and went back into the study.

There were two keys on a ring hanging on a hook near the back door. Sister Joan took them down and looked at them. When Mrs Fairly had gone out she would have slipped them into her handbag, but where was her handbag now? On impulse she turned and went up the stairs again. Perhaps in the panic after her death it had fallen down behind something. Getting down on hands and knees she peered under the bed and the other furniture but there was only the luggage she had packed up and her own empty bag.

She opened all the drawers again,

stood on a chair to peer into the recesses of the wardrobe shelf without finding anything. The handbag, if it had ever been there, had gone.

It was nearly time to walk across to the church for benediction. From the bedroom window she could see people drifting up the road. Probably more than usual, she mused with a touch of cynicism. Perhaps they hoped this Wednesday night benediction would be more dramatic than usual.

She went down the stairs in time to see both priests proceeding through the side door that led out of the parlour into the sacristy. Father Stephens was just ahead and behind him went Father Timothy. The latter's sandy hair was thinning on top and his bent head had a wry, tense aspect as if he forced himself to humility. She frowned, dismissing the notion. The truth was that something about the new priest — nearly everything about the new priest — irritated her.

"Always be respectful to priests for they are the Christ in our midst," Mother Agnes had counselled. "They are human, male and fallible but the office they hold dignifies them beyond the rest of us. It is the office and not the human being we honour."

Christ chose some unattractive representatives, she thought, and scolded herself as she went through into the study. Christ also chose some very unsuitable brides too if her own case was anything to go by.

The study window was closed, the newspaper spread out on the table. At the convent one newspaper was delivered once a month for the prioress to read and to decide if anything in it was to be imparted to her charges. Not until she had leaned over to scan it did she admit to herself that checking on the window had been only the second reason for coming in here.

Beneath the stark column the editors had seen fit to slip in a political cartoon. Something about law and order. Sister Joan grimaced as she perused the flat, hard phrases. On the northern line a body, mutilated beyond recognition, had been found lying by the side of the track. It was not yet known exactly how the victim, a young man, had come

136

by his terrible injuries. The public was asked to report if they had any pertinent information. The reporter had ended with a triple question: *Accident, suicide or murder?*

Surely not accident, she thought. The body had been stripped which a train could hardly have done. Would a suicide take off all his clothes in order to jump in front of a train?

At the side an opinion article called for more hospitals for the mentally ill. The political cartoon was sour and not amusing. Feeling distinctly cast down Sister Joan put on her cloak and went to benediction.

7

THE bed was comfortable, the bedroom warm and airy, the street quiet. Sister Joan had dreamed during her novitiate of comfortable beds and warm rooms but now that she had both it was impossible to sleep. The truth was that she missed the special aura of peace that came every night with the grand silence, missed the tiny sounds all about her that told her that her sisters were sleeping, missed the plain white walls of her cell. When she opened her eyes here a street light illumined the writhing roses and buttercups on the wallpaper. It was a relief when her internal alarm clock told her it was 4.30, the hour at which the lay sisters rose and summoned the other nuns to a new day. For a moment she was seized by the mischievous desire to yell the customary greeting of 'Christ is risen' to frighten the two slumbering Fathers, and scarcely had she turned over, her mouth quirking with laughter at the picture she had conjured up, than she fell into a heavy sleep from which she was roused by the anxious voice of Father Stephens outside the bedroom door.

"Sister Joan! Sister Joan, is everything all right?"

"Perfectly all right, Father. I'll be down in a few moments." She tried to sound as if she had been awake for hours, sliding from bed and grabbing at her habit and blinking at her fob watch which informed her it was nearly seven o'clock.

Washing and teeth would have to wait. She hurried on her clothes, snatched her cloak up and headed downstairs. It was, she thought, speeding down the front path and into the church where a couple of elderly women already knelt, an inauspicious start to the day. Father Stephens entered from the sacristy and she composed herself for the service.

Father Timothy would be up at the convent. She wondered if he'd stay to drink a cup of coffee with the sisters as Father Malone did. Probably not. Father Timothy was still too conscious of his vow of celibacy to feel at ease with women.

The Angel of the Presence dismissed, she sent up a quick prayer for a little extra help to get her through what she feared would be a difficult day and hurried out again. At least the bitter cold was warming under the emergence of a fragile young sun that gilded the tips of the young leaves and — oh no! Fully awake now she stopped dead at the front gate and stared in horror at the little garden where only the day before the border had been bright with the flowers of early spring. Not a bloom had escaped some slashing blade that had been wielded to such effect that the soil was littered with dying petals amid the desecrated stems.

"Sister, is something wrong?" Father Stephens, divested of his cassock, had opened the front door.

"The garden — " she said chokingly.

"Dear Lord! What happened here?" He came to meet her as she opened the gate, his handsome face drawn tight with shock and distaste. "Vandals! I hoped that we had been spared their

140

worst excesses here."

"Wouldn't vandals just pull them up by the roots and throw them around, Father?" she questioned. "These have been cut, the stems sliced through, and the heads piled up in the border."

"I believe you're right, Sister." He bent to look, then straightened up. "When you came out this morning — "

"I never looked at anything," she confessed. "I had overslept and I was only intent on getting to church on time."

"Here comes Father Timothy. Perhaps he noticed." Father Stephens waved impatiently as the car slowed to a stop.

"Good morning, Father. Sister Joan. I am about to garage the car before I come in for breakfast," Father Timothy said, putting his head out of the window and giving them both a wintry smile. "You've seen the damage then? I noticed it on my way out this morning but there wasn't time to inform you then. The offenders ought to be severely punished."

"Then it must have been done late last night." Father Stephens cast a frowning look at the border as Father Timothy drove on into the garage. "Come inside and start breakfast, Sister. No point in standing here."

He was right, of course. The damage was done and the routine of the day had to be followed. Sister Joan went into the kitchen, took off her cloak, and set about beating eggs with as much vigour as if the eggs themselves had offended.

When she took the scrambled eggs and toast into the dining-room both priests were at the table, Father Timothy putting a hand over his cup as she lifted the coffee pot.

"Just dry toast and a glass of water for me, Sister," he said.

"That's no kind of breakfast on which to start the day," Father Stephens said.

"It's my custom to abstain in Lent," Father Timothy said. "Naturally as my superior you are entitled to order me to eat."

"I'm sure Father Stephens wouldn't dream of interfering with your penitential practices, Father," Sister Joan said, holding her exasperation in check with difficulty. "You'll take some extra egg, Father? It turned out better than I expected, and the toast is nice and hot."

"Thank you, Sister." Father Stephens seemed to cheer up slightly as he looked at his plate. "I have been wondering if I ought not to inform the police about the damage. First the trees at the convent and then this — "

"Something happened at the convent?"

"Just before you arrived, Father. A large oak tree and several holly bushes were slashed and hacked," Father Stephens said. "Mother Prioress informed me about it. It was wanton destruction no less."

"Vandals," Father Timothy said and bit gloomily into a piece of dry toast.

"And no doubt the police have sufficient to occupy them." Father Stephens sighed. "If you see one of the constables, Sister, you can mention it to him, but there seems little point in making a specific report."

Mother Dorothy had thought it fruitless to report the incident. What would her advice be now? Sister Joan went into the kitchen, poured herself a coffee, and took an apple and a piece of toast. There was no apparent connection between the two events but the violence implicit in both was disturbing. Mother Dorothy, she reflected, would probably tell her to use her own judgement in the matter.

Meanwhile there were the dishes to be washed, the furniture to be polished, the border to be cleared before Mrs Fairly's niece arrived. She chewed the apple thoughtfully, finished her coffee, and rose, determined that the rest of the day was going to go smoothly.

"Leave our bedrooms until later, Sister." Father Stephens emerged from the study as she started up the staircase. "Miss Potter will be arriving later and I feel we ought to offer her a room for the night. Perhaps you will make up the guest room?"

"Yes, of course, Father. Will she be here for lunch?"

"I don't know, Sister. You had better make extra just in case."

"If it's a bit meagre," Sister Joan said meanly, "I'm sure Father Timothy won't mind going without."

"Father Timothy is an example to us all," Father Stephens said. He sounded, she thought, rather less inspired by it than he might have been.

The guest room was larger than the other rooms and had the faint chill of disuse about it. There were twin beds lacking bedding, a large wardrobe and chest of drawers and an armchair with slightly sagging cushions. A prayer stool and a bedside table completed the furnishings. The wallpaper, she noticed, had the same riotous roses and buttercups. Reminding herself to clear away the mess in the garden border she carried linen and blankets from the airing cupboard, made up one of the beds and flicked a duster over the surfaces. Some touch of welcome would be nice but since she had never met Sylvia Potter she couldn't make up her mind what would be appropriate. The other might prefer to go to an hotel anyway.

Opening the window to allow the fresh, cool air of the morning to circulate, she went briskly downstairs again. Cheese salad for lunch with fruit salad and cake to follow, she decided. Nothing to go cold and spoil there, and she could cheat a little by opening tins and buying the cake. She began clearing a surface on which to prepare the salad greens, brushing toast crumbs into the small pedal bin which was almost full. The remains of the breakfast eggs were decidedly unappetizing. Father Stephens hadn't, it seemed, been able to eat a double portion. She tied the top of the bin liner and went out into the back garden where the wheeled bin stood, ready to be left outside for the weekly collection.

Lifting the lid she slung in the bin liner and stood, holding the lid up, staring at the square brown paper parcel within. Someone had made an effort to push it down among the other refuse in the tied-up black bags. She had tilted the bin as she lifted the lid, dislodging the concealing bags. The probable sequence of events ran through her mind as she tugged out the parcel, put it under her arm, and went back into the kitchen. Tearing off the paper with its inadequate binding of sticky tape, dropping the wrapping into the small pedal bin, feeling no surprise at all as the shabby brown handbag was revealed.

The house was quiet. Both clerics had presumably departed on parish business. She took the bag upstairs, went into her room, and closed the door. It was her clear duty to inform the police what she had found and she had every intention of doing so, but first she wanted to look inside herself. It was no longer prying but investigation, she told herself firmly, as she unclasped the top and looked inside.

Two compartments were separated by a zipped section. She drew out the contents carefully. A cheque book, a plastic folder holding a library card and a bank card, a book of stamps, a birthday book with butterflies on the cover, a paying-in book, some clean tissues. Mrs Fairly had been neat and tidy to the utmost degree. Even the contents of her handbag could have been displayed for inspection. The cheque book had the amounts neatly dated and tabulated. The paying-in book recorded her monthly salary. The housekeeper had lived well within her means. She had a balance of £2,000 in her current account, no sign of any savings accounts. There was a purse containing two £5 notes and in the birthday book the names of Father Malone, Father Stephens and Sylvie were written opposite the requisite dates. The other pages were blank.

She unzipped the centre compartment carefully. A rosary and a St Christopher medal were inside, nothing else.

Sister Joan replaced the contents, turning each one over as she did so. If there had ever been anything of interest inside then it had been removed. In that case why wrap the bag in brown paper and push it down into the refuse bin? She sat on the edge of the bed, holding the bag, trying to fathom the actions that had led to its being discarded. No! not discarded! If the bag had simply been thrown out with the rubbish then it could easily have been put into one of the black bin liners. Instead it had been wrapped in brown paper and placed in the bin, to be taken out later. That could only mean that someone wanted to examine the bag more closely. Someone had had limited time or opportunity in which to find whatever it was they were seeking, and had hastily wrapped and cellotaped the bag and thrust it into the outside bin, meaning to return and retrieve it. The refuse wasn't due to be collected for another couple of days so there hadn't been any pressing urgency.

She thought a moment longer, lifted her pillow and put the handbag beneath, pulled up the coverlet and went downstairs again. Lifting the telephone receiver in the study, dialling the local police station, she kept her ears pricked for the sound of returning footsteps.

"I'm afraid Detective Sergeant Mill isn't coming in today, Sister. May I take a message for him or is there something I can do to help?"

The voice at the other end was bright and female. Sister Joan said, "No, it can wait. Thank you."

Sooner or later, she was certain, someone would go out to the refuse bin and reach down for the parcel. Someone would betray themselves. She stood a moment longer, then went swiftly back into the kitchen, fumbling in the cabinet drawer for brown paper and sticky tape, emptying a small cardboard box of its reels of cotton, hunting for a pen.

The police were hampered by regulations. Mother Dorothy had intimated that if, without breaking the rule, she could find a gentler verdict than suicide to pronounce over Mrs Fairly's memory then she was free to use her own initiative. And nowhere in the rule was it written that one wasn't permitted to set a trap for a murderer in order that justice might be served.

By the time Father Stephens walked into the presbytery the table had been laid and the salad prepared and Sister Joan was on her knees, removing the last few wilting heads of the destroyed flowers.

"Have you time to make me a coffee, Sister?" He paused at the front door.

"Yes, of course, Father." Getting to her feet she hurried towards him. He looked tired, she thought. Recent events had shaken him more than he cared to admit. "Is Father Timothy with you?"

"He went to the station to meet Miss Potter. I've been dealing with the first communicants."

"If you're not sure what time she's arriving — ?" Sister Joan looked at him.

150

"There are three trains from the north this morning. Father Timothy offered to meet them all. As he reminded me one can pray and meditate anywhere."

"I'll get your coffee, Father."

Putting on the kettle she tried to imagine how she would feel to have lost a beloved aunt and to be met at the end of a tiring journey by the joyless countenance of a strange priest.

"I need to go to the bakery, Father." She set the cup of coffee at his elbow. "I will need some money."

"Handbag not turned up yet? Here you are then." He took a couple of banknotes out of his wallet and gave them to her. "Father Malone deals with the financial side of things. If you require more let me know. Mrs Fairly kept an account book in the kitchen somewhere so you can enter your purchases later."

"I thought I'd buy some cake to go with the fruit for dessert," she said. "Would you like me to walk along to the station and see if there's any sign of Miss Potter yet?"

"That would be very good of you, Sister." He nodded absently, his fingers fluttering towards a sheaf of notes before him.

"Your Easter sermon?" she asked.

"I'm hoping to make it rather special."

She stood irresolute for a moment, longing to say, 'But the people don't want special sermons at such times, Father. Easter, like Christmas, is a link with childhood and innocence, a time to renew old traditions. People want simplicity, not clever argument and obscure references.'

"I'm sure it will be splendid, Father," she said kindly and left him to his musings.

Outside the pale sun had strengthened. She walked to the bakery and went in.

"I've a nice big treacle tart, Sister, or a plum pie." The girl behind the counter looked as if she sampled her own wares, her face dimpled and soft.

"The plum tart, please."

Sylvie Potter might have dentures and find treacle tart too sticky. She might also be allergic to plums, Sister Joan thought. Perhaps it would have been wiser to buy both. Sister Joan bit her lip, aware in some part of herself that it was much more comforting to worry about food than about the possibility of that other person who waited to retrieve the handbag from the refuse bin.

"Terrible about what happened, isn't it?" the girl behind the counter said.

"About Mrs Fairly, you mean? Yes, very sad."

"I was at benediction last evening. I saw you there."

"Oh, you're a member of the parish! I'm sorry. I can't seem to concentrate on any one thing for more than two minutes today," Sister Joan apologized.

"It was quite a shock." The girl slid the tart expertly into a cardboard case.

"Did you know her well?"

"Not really." The girl spun blue paper ribbon round the box and sliced it off neatly. "She was always very pleasant though. Very quiet and ladylike. Mind you, she didn't come from round here, you know. She and her husband came from up north. He took early retirement because of a bad heart and she used to clean and cook on a daily basis for Father Malone. Then her husband died and she went to live at the presbytery. Less lonely for her. And then the sisters came to the old Tarquin house and — mind you I was still at school then. I did think of becoming a nun myself at one time but it was just a passing fancy. No real vocation. No, have the tart on me, Sister. My Eddie owns the bakery now and he'd want me to show our respects under the circumstances."

"That's very kind of you," Sister Joan said gratefully.

"I'll tell you something for free, Sister." The other leaned her plump frame on the counter. "Mrs Fairly wouldn't have killed herself, not in a thousand years. She just wouldn't have done such a thing. Why, there was a man in here last year some time, trying to give out information on euthanasia and Mrs Fairly spoke up real sharp, told him life was a gift from God and He'd take it back when He was ready. She got quite angry about it. So she wouldn't have done it to herself, now would she?"

"I'm sure she didn't," Sister Joan said warmly. "Thank you for the tart. Mrs Fairly's niece is expected."

"And you won't be eating any of that yourself it's being Lent. That was one of the reasons I decided that the religious life wasn't for me. Too much penance and fasting."

"But excellent as a slimming diet," Sister Joan said with a twinkle.

Her spirits had lifted as she left the bakery. There were still nice, decent people in the world who cared about other people and didn't go round slashing at trees and innocent flowers and —

The body found by the side of the railway line had been mutilated, slashed, made less than human. The speeding train would inflict horrific injuries but would the victim have been flung to the side? She shivered, the brightness of her mood fading a little. There was almost certainly no connection between the events. All of them were symptoms of a darkness that needed to be fought.

The station was almost deserted save for the spare frame of Father Timothy who stood on the platform, peering anxiously up the track.

"Is there any sign of Miss Potter, Father?" Sister Joan joined him.

"The third train came in twenty minutes ago." He turned a worried face towards her, "And there was no sign of anyone called Miss Potter. I asked several ladies. Or are you here to tell me there's been another telephone call?"

"Not as far as I know. Father Stephens suggested I might come and find out if she had arrived."

"Not as far as I know."

"She may have rung up since I came out. The next train isn't until three or thereabouts. You can't wait here for ever."

"I shall come back this afternoon if there's been no word. I do feel she ought to have given us more information."

"I daresay she couldn't think very clearly," Sister Joan said. "She and her aunt were apparently very close."

"It is never wise to form close personal attachments, Sister." He spoke gravely as they left the station together. "God is jealous. He does not create us to form personal attachments. He creates us to serve Him only."

"But surely human affection can be a reflection of Divine Love," Sister Joan said.

"You would choose the shadow instead

of the substance? That is hardly what is expected of a religious," he reproved. "God alone fulfils our needs, Sister. Personal feelings must be rooted out with prayer and penitence. There is no other way."

As well try to argue with a stone, Sister Joan thought, compressing her lips and quickening her step. She was relieved when the open door of the presbytery came into sight and Father Stephens looked out.

"Miss Potter hasn't arrived," Sister Joan began.

"I know." Father Stephens looked pale and agitated. "I've just had a telephone call from the police. Apparently a young woman was found dead at the side of the railway line about an hour ago. They identified her by a note in her pocket giving this address — she was mutilated, you see."

8

"I HAVE been waiting at the station most of the morning," Father Timothy said. He sounded aggrieved.

"I only just received the telephone call," Father Stephens excused himself. "The police here were contacted by the railway police further up the line and, as my address was on the body, they naturally rang me. She had other means of identification on her."

"So she won't be eating the plum tart," Sister Joan said blankly. Both men looked at her.

"Surely food ought to be the last thing on our minds at this moment," Father Stephens said stiffly.

"I'm sorry, Father." She went past them, through to the kitchen and put the box carefully on the table.

Father Malone would have understood, she thought, how in moments of great drama the mind takes refuge in little things. The letter unwritten, the word unspoken, the plum tart uneaten — these had their own poignancy.

"I spoke somewhat sharply just now, Sister." Father Stephens hovered in the doorway. "When one is shocked one often says inappropriate things. Perhaps you would be kind enough to prepare some lunch? Afterwards I have to try to contact Miss Potter's home. She shared a house with another schoolteacher so I assume her friend will be asked to identify her. A most unpleasant task."

"Did the police say how it could have happened?"

"They assume she fell from the train. Some of these carriage doors fly open very easily."

"But the mutilations?" To keep her hands steady she held them tightly together within the comfort of her wide sleeves.

"She might have been caught by her clothing on the edge of the door and dragged. Naturally they'll be making extensive enquiries."

Nodding, he withdrew. She heard the slow, sombre tones of his voice speaking

159

to Father Timothy as they went into the study.

It hadn't been an accident. She was as sure of that as she was sure of anything in her life. Sylvia Potter had been killed. She had either been pushed from the train or attacked while she was travelling and thrown out on to the line. Someone had an interest in making sure that Mrs Fairly's niece didn't reach her destination.

She served the lunch, noticing that Father Timothy, apparently in response to a quelling glance from his fellow priest, ate the cheese salad and a slice of the plum tart without argument. Sister Joan stood in the kitchen, drinking the remains of the warmed over tomato soup and munching on a tired looking pear, her eyes on the back window through which she could see the square of concrete paving on which the wheeled refuse bin stood. Had she done the right thing or should she have waited for the return of Detective Sergeant Mill and told him? Strictly speaking, yes, but she guessed that the police officer would have vetoed her plan, adding a few pertinent remarks about bumbling amateurs for good measure.

"Sister, when you've washed up I'd like you to return to the convent." Father Stephens was in the doorway again.

"I'm sorry if my work doesn't satisfy you, Father." Her face had flushed.

"It isn't that at all, Sister. I have a number of books I promised to take up to Sister David for the purposes of her research. I shall be too busy this afternoon to take them and Father Timothy is taking the confirmation class for me, so if you don't mind driving up there — ?"

"Of course not, Father. Sorry I was so prickly."

"Recent events have rendered us all a little on edge," he allowed. "Perhaps you would acquaint Mother Dorothy with the latest developments. They are not of direct concern to the community but she likes to be kept up to date on parish affairs."

"Yes, Father." She rolled up her sleeves and plunged her hands into the hot water, feeling a curious, contradictory tugging. It would be a relief to her own nerves to spend a few quiet hours back in the enclosure but since she couldn't be in two places at once then the refuse bin would remain unwatched. Since there seemed no way round the quandary she decided to put it to the back of her mind. There was no point in fretting about something that couldn't be altered, and in any case, she fancied that whoever would go to the bin acted under the cloak of darkness whenever possible.

The dishes washed and left to drain she put on her cloak and went out to the garage. Under the cloak she held Mrs Fairly's handbag closely against her. Up at the convent she would have the opportunity to examine it more thoroughly without risk of being interrupted.

The presbytery car was nearly as dilapidated as the convent car. She drove with care up the street and turned on to the moorland track, feeling a sense of homecoming as she neared the schoolhouse, its windows now boarded up. Perhaps it would be wiser to examine the handbag here and then leave it somewhere for the police to pick up.

Suiting deed to thought she slowed, stopped, switched off the engine, and got out of the car. Around her the moor rose and dipped, the grass still winter short, the bracken brown and crackling. It was still cold but there was definitely spring on the way.

She sat down on a large tussock and opened the handbag again, taking out everything, turning it upside down and feeling round the lining for some tear that might conceal something. There was absolutely nothing beyond what she had already found. Certainly there was no reason why anybody should hide it in a refuse bin with the intention of retrieving it at a later date.

Nonplussed, she put back the contents, snapped it shut and got back into the car.

"'Morning, Sister!" Padraic Lee appeared suddenly from behind the schoolhouse.

"Padraic, were you spying on me?" She opened the door, tilting her head up at him.

"Picking some wild garlic, Sister, over yonder. I told Sister Perpetua that I'd seen a patch and would get some for the messes she brews up. Garlic's good for the heart and for winter colds. Bit of excitement down at the presbytery I hear."

"A very sad event," Sister Joan said. "Did you know Mrs Fairly?"

"Not to speak to." He shook his head, the gold rings in his ears glinting. "She's not like you nuns — too respectable to have truck with the Romanies."

Sister Joan's lips twitched at the backhanded compliment but she answered gravely, "It was a great shock to Father Stephens. Father Malone had already left on his pilgrimage. Unless it becomes absolutely necessary he won't be informed yet."

"Luther's in a bit of a taking." Padraic looked thoughtfully at his bundle of stalks and leaves. "Says he had no hand in the cutting of the trees."

"I'm quite sure that he didn't," Sister Joan said decidedly.

"But someone did." He cocked a black eyebrow at her.

"Yes. Someone did." She frowned down at the shabby handbag.

"And a respectable woman like Mrs Fairly doesn't kill herself," Padraic said.

"No. No, she doesn't."

"Are the sisters carrying handbags these days?" he asked.

"One day your curiosity will get you into hot water," she said. "This is Mrs Fairly's bag. I found it hidden in the refuse bin. There's nothing unusual in it."

"Hidden? Not thrown away?"

"I'm sure hidden. There's nothing in it that's suspicious or — I can't work it out."

"Would you like me to keep the bag for you, Sister?" he offered. "I can keep it in a safe place until the time comes for your wanting it again."

"Thank you, yes. That would be best, I think." She gave it to him with a feeling of relief. "Padraic, if anything happens — "

"Like what?"

"I don't know — anything. Will you see that Detective Sergeant Mill gets the bag?"

"Only for you, Sister," Padraic said, "would I consider going to the police."

"I'm sure it won't be necessary," she assured him.

"But you've a feeling something might." His black eyes were shrewd. "I hope you know what you're about, Sister."

"So do I," she said fervently. "Shall I take the garlic for Sister Perpetua?"

"Thanks, Sister." He handed it in to the car and stood back, tugging at the red muffler round his neck as he said awkwardly, "The school's sadly missed, Sister. That and your visits to the camp. Edith and Tabitha don't get on so well at big school and it's a long way to be driving them every morning."

"I'll ask Mother Dorothy for permission to visit you after Lent," she said. "How are things at home?"

"Not so bad, Sister. Not so bad at all." He answered as usual with an optimism that flew in the face of reality. Padraic's wife was an alcoholic and those who were inclined to look down on the swarthy scrap-metal dealer and regard him as an unfortunate relic of a despised race might have thought twice had they seen his ferociously clean caravan, the care he devoted to his children's manners and education.

Sister Perpetua was in the yard when she drove up, the freckled face breaking into a broad smile of welcome.

"Think of the devil! — well, not exactly, but I was just wondering how you were making out down at the presbytery," she said heartily. "Not that you're likely to be kept on for your cooking mind, but I've a notion Father Stephens might be hard to please."

"Not so far." Sister Joan alighted, wild garlic in hand. "I met Padraic on the way and he gave me these for you, together with his respects."

"That man is a joy and a godsend," Sister Perpetua said. "Mind, the year's early for the garlic but the young shoots are marvellous provided they've escaped the frost. So what's going on at the presbytery? We had prayers here for Mrs Fairly. Poor soul! she must have had a mental breakdown or something. I never met her more than once or twice myself but Father Malone always spoke highly of her."

By this time they were in the kitchen — large, stone flagged and blessedly familiar. Sister Teresa looked up with pleasure in her face from the knives and forks she was cleaning and from the infirmary Sister Gabrielle's hoarse old voice called, "Back like a bad penny, girl? Your cooking wasn't missed but you were."

"They like my cooking so well that they're thinking of keeping me on as a permanent fixture," Sister Joan declared, darting through to the old ladies.

"Then Father Stephens isn't the gourmet he pretends to be," Sister Gabrielle said. "You'd better make your report to Mother Dorothy but come in for a moment before you leave, won't you?"

"Yes, of course, Sister." Smiling, she hurried on to the parlour, taking off her cloak as she went.

"*Dominus vobiscum.*" Mother Dorothy looked up expectantly from her desk as Sister Joan came in.

"*Et cum spiritu tuo.*" Sister Joan knelt and took the stool her superior indicated.

"We didn't expect to see you so soon, Sister," Mother Dorothy said.

"Father Stephens asked me to bring over some books that Sister David requires for her research, Mother. They're in the back of the car. And he asked me to tell you what's been happening."

"Has anything been happening?" The other gave her a mild look.

"Mrs Fairly's niece, Sylvia Potter, was expected at the presbytery today. Father Timothy went down to the station to meet her but she didn't turn up. Father Stephens had a telephone call from the police telling him that she had been found dead at the side of the railway track a couple of stops up the line."

There was silence. Mother Dorothy's pale face had paled further but her voice was steady when she said, "She was quickly identified then?"

"She had identification on her and the address of the presbytery in her pocket so they rang the presbytery."

"How did she meet her death?" Mother Dorothy's face was very still. It was a sign that behind the small, impassive features her mind was working rapidly.

"They're still making enquiries," Sister Joan said. "It's only that — "

"Only that what, Sister?"

"You may not have seen a newspaper, Mother. There was a report in the one that was delivered to the presbytery to say that an unidentified man had been found, badly mutilated, by the side of the track on the northern line."

"Not in the same place?"

"No, Mother, much further north. I saw the headline when I took the newspaper into Father Stephens and I . . ."

"Couldn't resist reading the rest of it. In your case, Sister, that was only to be expected. Do you see any connection between the two?"

"I'm not sure, Mother. The first victim hasn't been identified yet. The body had been stripped."

"One would be tempted to lose faith in the essential goodness of creation if one were to read too many newspapers," Mother Dorothy said. "It sounds like a most unhappy coincidence. Miss Potter's death is very tragic though. Very sad indeed."

"Father Stephens is trying to contact the friend with whom she lived. That's why he didn't bring up the books himself."

"Then you had better give them to Sister David and you'll want to spend a little time in chapel before you drive back. I don't suppose that anyone has been interviewed for the post of housekeeper yet?"

"I don't think so, Mother."

"Well, I've given you one week's leave from the enclosure," Mother Dorothy said, "so if they haven't found anybody within that time then they will have to make shift to manage by themselves. I am of the opinion that a nun's place is in the convent and not gadding about at everybody's beck and call. You are not neglecting your spiritual duties?"

"I am trying not to," Sister Joan said honestly.

"Confine yourself to your housekeeping tasks then. I suppose there is no chance of Mrs Fairly's death having been an accident?"

"Detective Sergeant Mill believes that it wasn't suicide."

"Let us hope he is correct. If you were in the course of your duties and you were to chance upon something that strengthened that belief it would be your business then to acquaint him with it. I hope I make myself clear, Sister."

"Yes, Reverend Mother. Very clear."

She too had seen those films in which a double agent was sent out by MI5 with the words, "If anybody rumbles you then you're on your own. We shall simply deny all knowledge of you."

"May I look in on Sister Gabrielle and Sister Mary Concepta before I leave?" she asked.

"Yes, of course, Sister. And have a word with Sister Teresa too, will you? She looks a little troubled, I thought. Probably nothing important but she and you have worked together very amiably."

"Yes, Reverend Mother."

Rising, Sister Joan made her way across the hall into the chapel corridor. The chapel itself was silent, only the sanctuary lamp burning to remind those who came that the season of penance wouldn't last for ever. She knelt down in her customary place, blessed herself, and asked silently for some guidance. In her experience it was often better to send up a simple request and wait for the answer which always came though not always in the manner one expected.

Her petition winging on its way she rose and went up the stairs into the library. During Lent secular books were not read and Sister David used the breathing space to rebind, to check on stocks. She was here now, carefully pasting in small cards inside the front covers, her little rabbit face intent on her task.

"Sister David?"

"Sister Joan, how nice to see you here!" The other looked up with genuine pleasure in her face.

Sister David wasn't the easiest of the community with whom to get along. She was inclined to pedantry and any sense of humour she might have possessed was well hidden. But there was something touchingly sweet about her earnestness.

"Father Stephens sent me over with the books you needed for your project," Sister Joan said. "They're on the back seat of the car. Would you like to come down and we'll carry them up?"

"Oh, I can manage them, Sister. How kind of Father to remember. He must have so many extra duties too since Father Malone went — no, I shall manage perfectly. Thank you."

She darted out, her sharp little nose positively quivering with eagerness. Sister Joan smiled after her and went on into the storeroom. If there had been time she would have spent half an hour sorting out the newspaper clippings for her scrapbook of the history of the district, but time was limited if she was to get back to the presbytery and make supper. Nevertheless she went over to the table and looked down at the neat piles of clippings.

Someone had moved them. Not only moved them but also muddled them up. Irritated, she ruffled through a couple of the piles, seeing that not only days but years had been transposed. Someone had gone through the clippings, and clipped the piles together again at random.

There wasn't time to do anything about it now, and in any case it would be quite useless to try to guess if anything had been removed. She left the cuttings where they were and went back to the library as Sister David returned, books piled to her chin.

"You should have let me help you, Sister." Sister Joan hastened to relieve her of her burden.

"Oh no, Sister." Sister David pushed her spectacles higher on her nose. "It gives me real pleasure to be able to see and touch books that they seem quite light when one comes to carry them! I couldn't have asked for a better selection."

"How is your work going?" Sister Joan asked.

"Slowly but surely." Sister David flushed a little. "Of course one cannot spend too much time on it during Lent but eventually if it does find a publisher then the community will benefit quite considerably. At least one trusts so."

"And you might find yourself famous, Sister."

"Oh, God forbid!" Sister David said with genuine horror. "That would be dreadful! Having one's name known and reporters coming and — oh, I couldn't bear that! No, I shall publish it anonymously of course."

"Sister, has anyone been up here recently?" Sister Joan changed the subject somewhat abruptly, feeling as usual inadequate in the face of real humility.

"Not to borrow any books, Sister. Not during Lent. Some of the sisters have brought books back, of course."

"So someone could have come up here?"

"Why, yes, Sister, at any time, I suppose." Sister David looked bewildered. "But why would they?"

"Some of the newspaper cuttings I was sorting out have been disturbed."

"The cuttings for the scrapbook? Oh, that's dreadful!" Sister David stared at her. "I hope that you don't think that I — I would never do such a thing!"

"No, of course I don't," Sister Joan said warmly. "As you say anyone could have slipped up and taken a look and — muddled them. There's no need to mention it. I don't suppose that it's important."

"But nobody has the right to meddle with someone else's papers," Sister David said, distressed.

"It's not important," Sister Joan repeated.

Going downstairs again she wondered

if the rule of not meddling also applied to the possessions of the dead. Perhaps it was justified when one was trying to find out the truth.

Sister Teresa was in the enclosed part of the visitors' parlour, cleaning the grille that separated it from the part where visitors from outside the convent could enter through a side door that opened on to the garden and sit chatting for the permitted twenty minutes.

"Sister, how are things going?" Sister Joan entered the parlour and sat down on one of the two stools there.

"Oh, all the sisters are being very helpful," Sister Teresa said. Her eyes were downcast and there was something evasive in her voice. Sister Joan, glancing at her sharply, decided that Reverend Mother had reason for concern. Teresa was a sturdy young woman whose placid manner and rosy cheeks betokened a contented nature and a healthy body. Today she looked pale and there were shadows beneath her eyes.

"You're not driving yourself too hard?" she queried anxiously. "I think it was Saint Clare who told her nuns not to be too hard on themselves because bodies aren't made of brass. You're not fasting beyond the rule?"

It was not, she reflected, any of her business but Mother Dorothy had requested her to have a quiet word, and Sister Teresa answered docilely, "No, Sister. I eat everything that's allowed."

"In just over a year you'll be a fully professed member of the community," Sister Joan said cheerfully, wondering if the trouble lay in the spiritual realm. "You must be feeling rather nervous at the prospect of a year's seclusion but it isn't as bad as one always imagines. Mother Dorothy and Father Malone will be talking to you and Sister Hilaria, of course, and the rest of us will be praying for you."

"Oh, going into seclusion doesn't trouble me," Sister Teresa said. "It will give me the chance to look into my own heart before making the final commitment."

"But something is troubling you."

"Sister Joan, if someone you knew was doing something against the rule,

178

something very much against the rule, and you weren't yet fully professed, what would you do?" Sister Teresa blurted.

"Does this breach of the rule involve cruelty or distress to anybody else?"

"No. No, I don't think so. Nobody else knows about it except me. They're all asl — " Sister Teresa bit off the last word, looking painfully guilty.

"You know sometimes the rule can be interpreted in a fairly relaxed way," Sister Joan said carefully. "When I had to ride Lilith to the schoolhouse every day Mother Dorothy allowed me to wear jeans under my habit. If it is medically advised a sister is permitted to eat meat for a period. These are all matters decided between the nun and her prioress."

"Surely a sister wouldn't be allowed to go out walking all night!"

"Out walking? You mean when the rest of the community is asleep? After the grand silence?"

"I can't help but hear the back door being unbolted," Sister Teresa said, looking miserable. "The first night just for an hour, but last night it was nearly

179

time to get up again before Sis — the person returned."

"You're talking about Sister Jerome, of course? She sleeps in the cell next to yours just off the kitchen."

"I do hate telling tales." Sister Teresa looked uncannily like the schoolgirl she must have been not many years before.

"Nobody likes a snitch," Sister Joan agreed, "but when the rule is flouted then it is a big temptation to say something if only to prevent one's Sister in Christ from falling into sin. It doesn't mean we're being spiteful."

"You'll not say anything?" Sister Teresa looked imploring.

"Have you asked Sister Jerome why she goes out at night?"

"Sister Jerome isn't the kind of person one can easily ask."

"No. No, she isn't." Sister Joan gnawed at her lower lip for a moment. "Where is she now?"

"She went out mid-morning," Sister Teresa said. "She had leave to drive down into town to see the doctor there. Mother Dorothy gave her some things to buy — candles and polish and so on, and some garden tools, so she had quite a lot to do."

"Even though she's sick?"

"I don't think she's sick, Sister. She goes regularly to a doctor for some medicine or other, and as she's only just come here she'll need to sign on with a new doctor."

"Well, leave it with me." Sister Joan endeavoured to sound casual. "I'll have a word with her if I see her — don't worry, I'll keep your name out of it. She may have leave to perform some unusual, and private penance, you know, so I'd put it out of my head if I were you."

"Thank you, Sister." The other looked marginally happier.

"And I have to go or Father Stephens will be screaming for his supper. Do you know what medicine Sister Jerome takes? Another time I could pick it up for her myself."

"Valium," said Sister Teresa. "She takes a Valium before every meal. Sister Perpetua reckons that at the rate she takes them she must get through bottles of the stuff."

9

WHAT she needed to do was to find somewhere quiet where she could sit down and sort out the information she had into some kind of coherent order. For the moment however that was a luxury she couldn't afford. She said reassuringly if inaccurately to Sister Teresa, "There, you see! Poor Sister Jerome suffers from insomnia. That's probably why she was prescribed Valium in the first place. There's nothing to worry your head about."

She went out into the passage briskly, wondering if that particular drug was ever prescribed for insomnia. Her own experience of medication was limited to an occasional aspirin and Sister Perpetua's cough mixture. She had, however, set Sister Teresa's mind at rest for the moment.

"Are you going back now, Sister?" Sister Mary Concepta's voice drifted plaintively out of the infirmary.

"Very soon, Sister, but I have a few minutes." Sister Joan went into the warm, pleasant room where the two old ladies were living the long twilight of their old age, spending much of their time in the two basket chairs by the winter fire but still managing to get to most of the devotions and even, on occasion, to get up the stairs to eat and join in the recreation.

"Don't do us any favours, girl." Sister Gabrielle spoke crustily, her eyes holding a decided twinkle. "You're probably longing to get back to the fleshpots of the outside world."

"Take no notice of her, Sister. She's only teasing you," Sister Mary Concepta said.

"Good heavens, Mary Concepta, the child knows that!" Sister Gabrielle said.

"And there aren't many fleshpots around the presbytery," Sister Joan added.

"Not with that new priest there," Sister Gabrielle said, her grin stretching into a grimace. "I never saw such a joyless creature in my life. All starch and no smile."

"Sister, he is a priest," Sister Mary Concepta gently reproached.

"I wasn't under the impression he was a rabbi," Sister Gabrielle said, looking pleased with her own wit. "I've known priests of all shapes and conditions in my life and this one doesn't please me at all. He trotted in here after mass this morning and told us that it wouldn't be very long before we were released from our earthly exile."

"Well, I suppose that it's true," Sister Mary Concepta said.

"Of course it's true," Sister Gabrielle said impatiently, "but I don't need to be reminded of it. Sister Joan, hand me my stick and I'll walk out with you to the car."

Sister Joan did as she was bade wondering if the old lady were merely indulging a whim or if she had something private to say. It was evidently the latter since, the moment the back door had closed, the other said, "Suicide, accident or have you hit upon a murder?"

"There has been a murder," Sister Joan said. "A body was found on the railway track, unidentified; a man apparently who'd been stripped naked and was very badly mutilated."

"What has that to do with the housekeeper?"

"Her niece, a Miss Potter, was expected today. Father Timothy waited for hours at the station but she never turned up. Meanwhile Father Stephens had a message telling him her body had been found at the side of the railway track, a few miles up the line."

"In the same condition?"

"Mutilated but not stripped," Sister Joan said tersely. "It's possible she fell and was dragged along. They don't know yet."

"Sister Jerome sleeps badly," Sister Gabrielle said. "I don't sleep so well myself and I hear her walking, walking. It bothers me to see a fellow religious in trouble, but she's not the type to invite confidences. She's out today else I'd suggest you had a word with her."

"She's hardly likely to confide in me," Sister Joan said.

"Don't underestimate yourself, girl. You're the kind of person that people do confide in," Sister Gabrielle said unexpectedly. "You look sympathetic, you see, and as if nothing in the world could shock you. Yes, she might talk to you. There's some great burden that woman carries and it'd be well to get it out of the way."

"It'll have to wait. I've supper to cook." Sister Joan eased herself into the car.

"You know if I'm ever tempted to take Father Timothy down a peg or two," Sister Gabrielle said, "I restrain myself by remembering that he has to eat your cooking and that's penance enough for anybody. Go with God, girl, and come back safely."

"Thank you, Sister." Sister Joan drove slowly out of the yard.

She was near the main gates when she heard an excited yelping and slammed on the brakes in time to stop herself from running over the gambolling Alice who bounded round, her feathery tail wagging, her plump little body wriggling with joy as Sister Joan got out of the car.

"I hope you recognize me and don't greet everybody like that," she scolded.

"You are training to be a guard dog."

"She's young yet." Sister Jerome spoke in unwontedly mild tones as she came through the gates.

"Good afternoon, Sister Jerome." Sister Joan straightened up, summoning a smile.

"I have been into town," Sister Jerome said. "One has to sign on with a new doctor whenever one moves these days and they insist on a health check. Then I had to go to the next town because they didn't have the gardening tools that Sister Martha required."

"It must have been a tiring day, Sister," Sister Joan said, wondering why the other was troubling to explain her movements.

"I'm not complaining about it," Sister Jerome said, returning to her usual sullen manner. "One isn't put on this earth to fritter away one's time in idle pleasures. Even the dog will have to learn that."

"Surely you didn't walk up from town!" Sister Joan looked at the large, bulging bags the other was carrying.

"Reverend Mother instructed me to take a taxi," Sister Jerome said. "I dismissed it before we reached the gates. Money, like time, ought not, to be squandered."

"No, Sister, of course not."

It was impossible to like the woman, to feel the slightest warmth towards her, Sister Joan thought in despair. She stood there, weighed down by the heavy bags, her large white face impassive, her eyes hard and flat ringed with dark shadows.

"You don't look well, Sister." She spoke impulsively. "Are you settling in at the convent? The first few days in a strange place can sometimes be difficult. I remember when I first came — "

"One does not expect to be influenced by one's surroundings to any great extent," Sister Jerome said quellingly. "The interior life is what matters, Sister. Come, Alice!"

She walked on up the drive with Alice immediately deserting Sister Joan and trotting obediently at her side.

"You were wrong, Sister Gabrielle," Sister Joan muttered, getting back into the car. "I am not the sort of person that some people would ever confide in!"

And part of her irritation, she admitted

ruefully as she drove back to the presbytery, was due to the fact that Alice had gone off so happily without a backward look!

"Take the beam out of your own eye, dear, before you start fretting about the mote in your brother's," she admonished herself under her breath as she drove into the garage at the side of the church.

She would have liked to spend a few minutes in the church but Father Stephens was at the front door and she hurried up the path.

"There you are, Sister. No trouble with the car, I hope? No scrapes or scratches?" In Father Stephens's world females couldn't drive past a road sign without knocking it over.

"I managed beautifully, Father. Sister David was most grateful for the books. She asked me to thank you."

"I started supper, Sister." He hovered by the kitchen door as she went in. "Not that you're late but you do seem to have rather a lot to do, so I took the liberty."

"That was very kind indeed of you, Father!" Sister Joan looked in dismay at the enormous pan simmering on the cooker. From its size she guessed that Father Stephens had used up every vegetable in the place. "Stew, is it?"

"Just vegetables, Sister. I thought we might sprinkle a little grated cheese on top when it's brought to table. With some bread it ought to be very tasty."

"It looks as if you made sufficient for tomorrow too," she commented.

"Yes, it can be heated over," he agreed. "I managed to contact Miss Potter's friend. A young lady called Stephanie Hugh — a fellow schoolteacher. She is arriving on the late train. Not a Catholic, by the way, but she accepted my invitation to stay here so the guest room will be used after all."

"If she's not a Catholic perhaps I ought to meet her," Sister Joan said. "I mean she may not feel at ease with a priest."

Even the most fervent Catholic might have found it hard to be at ease with Father Timothy but she managed not to say so.

"That's very kind of you, Sister. Perhaps you can go after supper. I enquired of Miss Hugh if she would like a meal prepared but she said she was eating on the train."

Sister Joan, going to taste the vegetables and finding them unexpectedly good, hoped that Miss Hugh would have the good sense to travel in a crowded compartment and keep away from train doors.

She served the stew to the two clerics, receiving a courteous thank you from the one and a curt nod from Father Timothy who had just come through from the sacristy, ate her own portion in the kitchen, and slipped out into the back yard. In the gathering darkness of evening the wheeled refuse bin crouched like some robotic beast.

"Sister Joan!"

Father Stephens stood on the back step, peering out. There was no time to lift the lid and find out if the substitute parcel had gone.

"I was just taking a breath of air," she said quickly. "Did you want second helpings, Father?"

"I am not so fond of my own cooking as all that," he said, chuckling at his own small joke. "No, I think you ought to start out fairly soon for the station, in case Miss Hugh takes an earlier train. I'd not want her to arrive at a strange town with nobody there to meet her."

Or the wrong person waiting in the shadows? It would do no good to ask him. Father Stephens believed the least said the sooner something was mended.

"I'll go at once, Father," she said. "Will you have your coffee later then?"

"Yes, when Miss Hugh arrives. Thank you, Sister."

He was holding open the door for her and there was no excuse to linger. She went inside and put on her cloak again, took the keys from the hook by the door and went out.

At least she had been given leisure in which to think. She made good use of the ten minutes it took to cross the streets towards the station. Head bent into the wind, arms shrouded by her cloak, she banished the surroundings with the latecomers on their way home, the street lights casting pale pools of light on the road, and itemized events in her mind.

A body had been found by the side of

the railway track — stripped, mutilated, unidentifiable. Further down the track another body had been found, clothed, and easily identified. Near the postulancy trees had been slashed and chopped and in the border of the presbytery garden the spring flowers had all lost their brave, bright heads. Mrs Fairly had wanted to speak to her about the new lay sister up at the convent, that same sister who repelled any overtures of friendship and went out at night. Went out during the day too, Sister Joan reminded herself. Granted she had gone with permission to see the doctor, to buy some articles for the community, but she had gone further afield to buy the gardening implements. Sister Joan stopped dead, mentally kicking herself for not having asked a simple question.

Sister Jerome had driven into town in the convent car but she had taken a taxi back to the convent. So where had she left the convent car and why? Had the car broken down or had she had some sort of accident in it? She'd shown no trace of anything having happened but Sister Jerome had one of those faces one sees at a poker table.

She had reached the station. A few teenagers stood round the machine that dispensed chocolate. A nice bar of nutty milk chocolate would have been just perfect at this moment, she thought, and hastened her step on to the platform. There were a few people waiting here too, looking curiously lost on the almost deserted platform.

Sister Joan walked to the end and sat down on the bench there. The next train was due in twenty minutes and then there was a fairly long wait. She wondered if she would be justified in getting herself a cup of coffee. Probably not since there would be a cup available when she got back to the presbytery.

"It's Sister Joan, isn't it?" Someone had paused to look at her more closely.

"Constable Petrie! I have the money for the groceries for you." She fumbled for her purse but he shook his head.

"Tell Father Stephens that it's on me. I popped in to get a quick cup of coffee though I'm actually on duty."

"I won't tell," she said solemnly.

"Are you meeting someone, Sister?"

He sipped from the plastic mug he was holding. "Oh, I'm sorry. Would you fancy a coffee? It's not very good."

"Not for me, thank you. I'm waiting for Miss Hugh. She was Miss Potter's friend, a fellow schoolteacher — Miss Potter was Mrs Fairly's niece."

"Bad business that!" He frowned. "Bad business in both cases. You've heard the latest?"

"I've heard nothing."

"The doctor up at the hospital took a closer look at Mrs Fairly's body. She had a needle mark on her wrist and a bit of a bruise as if someone had held her arm very tightly."

"Detective Sergeant Mill told me about the needle mark."

"He was off up north today making a few enquiries," Constable Petrie said. "Anyhow up at the hospital the pathologist made some further tests — he found insulin."

"What?!" Sister Joan sat up straighter. "Insulin?"

"That stuff some diabetics have to inject themselves with to avoid going into a coma," he said.

"Yes, I know. Was Mrs Fairly diabetic?"

"Not according to her medical record," Constable Petrie said. "It looks like she only gulped a mouthful of the tea with the Valium in it, enough to make her feel whoosy, they reckon, and then she was pumped full of insulin. It was the insulin that killed her, not the drug. Seems a funny way of committing suicide."

"You don't still believe she killed herself?"

"No, Sister. I was on the telephone earlier to Detective Sergeant Mill and he said the result didn't surprise him. He reckons that someone spiked her late-night tipple, but the taste must have been pretty foul so she didn't drink it all and then someone went into the room just as she was starting to feel dizzy and injected the insulin. She probably didn't have time to struggle or cry out."

"And then the — person threw away what she hadn't drunk and left sufficient residue in the cup for everybody to think she'd died from the effects of the overdose."

Sister Joan shivered suddenly, thinking of the scene. Not wanting to think of the scene because it had a horror pervading it that made her feel physically ill.

"I didn't mean to upset you, Sister," he said quickly. "Look, let me get you a cup of coffee. Warm you up a bit."

"Thank you, that's very kind of you." She sat motionless until he came back with another plastic mug.

"You drink it down, Sister. You know, with being on the force, and with your good self having helped us before, I'm inclined to forget that you're not used to this kind of thing. I've had to develop the objective approach."

"Does anybody get used to murder?" she asked, gulping the hot, oversweet liquid.

"Probably not, Sister," he agreed, "but this ties in with Miss Potter's death, don't you see?"

"She obviously didn't fall out of the train," Sister Joan said. "Thank you for the coffee. I needed it."

"Train's about due." He took the empty mugs. "I'd better get back to the squad car, see if there are any messages. You'll be all right, Sister?"

"Perfectly all right," she assured him.

"Am I to tell Miss Hugh what has been found out?"

"Better let it lie until it's all official, Sister." He saluted her smartly as if, she thought with a spasm of amusement, she were a senior member of the force, and went off towards the exit.

The signals were intimating the approach of the train. Composing her face which must, she feared, still bear the imprint of shock, she rose, and stood poised, waiting.

"Sister Joan! Sister Joan!"

Constable Petrie was loping back into the station, his voice urgent. One or two of the others waiting on the platform turned to look at him.

"What is it?"

"Could you come out to the car for a moment, Sister?"

"The train's coming in. Miss Hugh may be on it."

"Right now, Sister. If you please?" He sounded official suddenly as if he were about to arrest her.

She went without further argument, hearing as she left the platform the onward rush of the approaching train.

"There was a message from the station," he said as they got into the squad car.

"Yes?" Sister Joan reached for the seat belt automatically.

"Seems they've found another body, Sister. When I told Detective Sergeant Mill that I had just been talking to you he asked me to bring you along."

"Another — ?" Sister Joan closed her eyes briefly while she endeavoured to control her voice. "Did he say who it was?"

"A young woman called Stephanie Hugh according to the identification she had on her."

"But I'm meeting her off the train," Sister Joan said stupidly.

"Yes, Sister. You told me." He swung the car out of the parking space.

"How did she — ?"

"I don't know yet, Sister. Detective Sergeant Mill said he'd fill me in on the details when we got there."

"Where is there?" She was struggling to regain her composure, to take in the fact that the woman she had been expecting to meet was dead. Suddenly and ruthlessly dead, for it was beyond the bounds of possibility that this death was a natural one.

"On the outskirts of town, Sister. We'll be there in a few minutes."

She nodded, biting her lip, her hands tensely locked together beneath the folds of her cloak. They had left the main street and were turning into a long steep side road, with houses dotted along it and a garage at the top.

Another police car was drawn up in the forecourt of the garage and an ambulance was pulling in. A man in overalls stood engrossed in conversation with the tall, familiar figure of Detective Sergeant Mill.

"Petrie, glad you got here so fast." He broke off his conversation and came to the side of the car. "The photographer's already here and the fingerprint people are on their way. Make sure that nothing is moved until all the usual routine's been followed, will you? Sister Joan, thank you for coming. Petrie mentioned that he'd been talking with you just before I contacted him."

"I was waiting for the train." She alighted from the car and moved with him towards the brightly lit façade of the garage.

"You went to meet Miss Hugh, Miss Potter's friend?"

"Father Stephens invited her to stay at the presbytery. Why are we here at this garage?"

"Miss Hugh's body was found here," he said.

"When? How?!" Bewildered she looked up at him. "I don't know why but I expected her — no, of course, I didn't expect a body until Constable Petrie told me — but after he told me I pictured it as lying by the railway track like the other two."

"The owner of the garage is short staffed this week," Detective Sergeant Mill said. "He closed the garage at six and went off home for a meal. When he came back at seven he decided to start work on a car that had been left here earlier today for some minor repairs. He worked on it for a bit and then he noticed the boot was unlocked. He opened it and — she was bundled inside it. He rang the police at once and I'd just walked into the station when the call came so I grabbed a car and drove out here immediately. The young woman had cheque book and address book in her handbag, so it seems fairly clear that she is Stephanie Hugh."

"Is it possible to identify her otherwise?" Sister Joan asked steadily.

"She was killed by a blow to the back of the head," he told her. "Looks as if someone took a swing at her with an axe but her face is undamaged. You never met her?"

"I've seen a photograph of Miss Potter taken when she was a schoolgirl but I never met either of them. I'd be unable to identify — "

"That wasn't why I asked Petrie to bring you along," he broke in. "Sister, the garage owner didn't recognize the car she was in but I did. She's hidden in the boot of the old car you sisters drive at the convent. One of the other sisters brought it in earlier because the clutch was going. She left it at the garage and phoned for a taxi to take her the rest of the way back. Can you tell me anything to throw light on this?"

10

FOR a moment she was silent, thoughts spinning in her head. Then she said, "The new lay sister at the convent, Sister Jerome, spent much of today out of the enclosure. She had to register with a new doctor and buy several things — gardening tools mainly — that were needed by Sister Martha. She took the car."

"You've been up to the convent today?"

"I took some books over that Father Stephens had promised to lend to Sister David. I was on my way back to town when I met Sister Jerome coming in just outside the main gates."

"Both of you being in cars?"

"I was driving the car from the presbytery. Sister Jerome was on foot. She'd paid off the taxi before reaching the convent gates in order to save money. She didn't mention having had any trouble with the convent car but then I didn't think to ask and we only exchanged a few words."

"What is she like — this Sister Jerome?"

"Not easy to get to know," Sister Joan said, adding fairly, "but then I've had very little contact with her since I went down to help out at the presbytery so soon after she arrived."

"And you never met Miss Potter or Miss Hugh, of course." He frowned.

"No. You don't want me to?" She nodded towards the garage, her face tense.

"That won't be necessary, Sister. I'll have to talk to Sister Jerome but that can wait until the morning."

"It will have to wait," she reminded him. "The grand silence starts at nine-thirty."

"How do you manage down at the presbytery?" he asked curiously.

"About the grand silence? I keep it as far as I can, but if I'm required to speak then I do so. The rule has to be applied intelligently, you know, and not followed slavishly."

"Yes, Sister." There was a faint smile on his face.

"Sorry, I didn't mean to give you a lecture," she said, smiling back.

"Give me a moment to have a word with the team here and I'll drive you back to the presbytery. May I leave it to you to break the news to Father Stephens?"

"Yes, of course."

She stood quietly as he strode away. Arc lights had been erected for the police photographer and two ambulance attendants had gone in with a stretcher. Poor Stephanie Hugh was arriving in a manner she couldn't possibly have envisaged.

"Petrie will keep an eye on things here," Detective Sergeant Mill said, returning to her side. "Come on and I'll give you a lift back."

Getting into his patrol car, fastening her seat belt, she framed a request.

"I'm wondering if it might be possible for me to talk to Sister Jerome. She may clam up if she's suddenly confronted by a police officer."

"Why should she if she hasn't anything to hide?" he demanded.

"Oh, come on now!" she expostulated. "Nuns simply aren't used to being involved no matter how innocently in something like this. And we all have something to hide. As soon as we are faced with questioning old guilts about completely unrelated matters come flooding into our minds. You must know that."

"I can't imagine you'd have anything to hide, Sister."

"Oh, I wasn't born wearing a habit and veil," she said lightly. "Mind you, I've never done anything truly dreadful but then who are we to weigh our sins? That's why Lent is so useful — to try to redress the balance a little bit. Sorry! I'm lecturing again. I never used to — it must be old age creeping on or something. Detective Sergeant, you went up north today. Was it to find out if there was any connection between the body found by the railway track there and Miss Potter's body?"

"Exactly that." He nodded approval. "I could have had the information phoned or faxed to me but I was due for a day off and I wanted to spend a couple of hours sniffing around the problem. The local police were very cooperative but they still haven't identified the victim. They think it likely that he was on his way to catch a train when he was lured into a nearby tunnel — there's a bit of disused line there, and killed. You wouldn't have wanted to see the extent of the injuries, Sister."

"And then stripped?"

"And then stripped. There must have been a lot of blood on his clothes. On the clothes of his assailant too. They'll find out who the poor devil was. Dental checks, reconstruction of the facial features, but it takes time."

"Is there a serial killer going round? A psychopath?"

"That's the general trend of thinking. I don't go all the way with it myself."

"Surely anyone who'd commit such deeds must be mentally deranged?" Sister Joan objected.

"Oh, certainly, but the average serial killer kills for the pleasure of killing, to release some dreadful inner tension, to achieve a sense of power — that sort of thing. And he uses the same method every time. He also wants unconsciously to boast of his cleverness so he sends tape recordings, writes letters to the police or to the newspapers. If these deaths are all connected, and I've a feeling that they are, then he doesn't kill at random. He picks his victims very carefully and he uses the most convenient method available at the time."

"An axe?" She shivered slightly.

"A short-handled axe and possibly a hammer as well. The injuries on the first victim suggest that. But Mrs Fairly was slipped a dose of Valium in her tea and whisky, and then injected with insulin. We might have missed that altogether if you hadn't been so certain that she hadn't committed suicide."

"But Sylvia Potter and Stephanie Hugh were killed with an axe again?"

"One hard blow with the cutting edge," he said briefly. "There would have been very little blood in both cases. Miss Potter was probably killed while she was on the train and then pushed out while the train was slowing down as it went round the bend. I don't know about Miss Hugh yet."

"And no attempt was made to hide their identities."

"None at all."

"Then perhaps the first one wasn't connected to the others?"

"Which gives us two people running round with the same or an identical weapon. My instinct tells me that isn't so."

They were at the end of the road, the bulk of the church looming up ahead. She experienced a sudden longing to jump out of the car and run into the sanctuary, to wash her hands of the events taking place around her.

"I think your instinct tells you rightly," she said. "Would you stop here, please? I don't want to alarm Father Stephens by being brought home in a police car."

He slowed and stopped, turning his head to look at her in the light from the dashboard.

"I'll delay my visit to the convent until late tomorrow morning," he said. "You'll have a word with Sister Jerome?"

"Yes, of course. Thank you."

"And you'll tell me if you have any information for me?" His glance was too keen. She fiddled with the unclasping of the seat belt before she answered.

"I may have some fresh information for you already, but first I must obtain Mother Dorothy's permission to tell you since she has given instructions it's not to be mentioned. I'm sure that in the light of recent events she'll rescind the order."

"If she realizes that she may be withholding valuable information then I am sure she will," he said. "Is that everything then, Sister?"

There was the handbag, she thought, now safely bestowed with Padraic Lee and the parcel she had wrapped up so neatly and thrust back into the refuse bin, but if she talked about those then he would insist that she abandon her plan.

"There isn't anything else for the moment, Detective Sergeant Mill," she said formally.

"Very well, Sister. Goodnight then. I'm sorry your day has ended so unpleasantly. You'll inform Father Stephens?"

"Yes, of course. Goodnight."

Getting out of the car she walked rapidly to the presbytery gate, glancing back as she turned in at the path and seeing that the car was still there. Did

Detective Sergeant Mill believe there was danger for her too or was he mentally scolding her for being unforthcoming?

She let herself in and went through to the dining-room where the two priests sat with a pot of coffee between them.

"I made the coffee for all of us, Sister." Father Stephens looked up expectantly. "Oh, didn't you wait for the later train?"

"Miss Hugh won't be coming, Father." Sister Joan said.

She had spoken quietly but something in her expression or attitude must have alerted him because he half rose from his place, darted a look at Father Timothy, and said, "Sit down, Sister, and I'll pour you a cup of coffee. You have bad news?"

"Very bad, Father." She accepted the chair and the coffee without argument. "She must have either left the train before the proper stop or caught an earlier one or perhaps — I don't know yet what happened. Her body was found in the boot of a car in a garage on the outskirts of town. Constable Petrie very kindly told me of it."

"Dear God!" Father Stephens said

softly, sitting down again abruptly. "Dear God, but what is going on? Mrs Fairly, Miss Potter, Miss Hugh — that recent terrible business up north — the world's run mad."

"When discipline fails then anarchy takes over," Father Timothy said. His face was grey-white and he spoke hoarsely.

"Detective Sergeant Mill believes all the deaths are connected," Sister Joan said.

"But how can they be?" Father Stephens looked puzzled.

"I don't know, Father. It's just a hunch he has." She drank the coffee, hardly realizing that it was a vast improvement on the station coffee until she had almost drained the cup.

"It must be near your grand silence, Sister," Father Timothy said. "You'll be glad of a rest, I daresay."

His tone was kinder than usual even if he did contrive to make it sound as she had wearied them out with chattering.

"You'd better get to your bed, Sister. Father and I can deal with the cups," Father Stephens said.

"I'll rinse them out and wash

them properly in the morning," she compromised, rising and piling them on a tray. "Good night, Father Stephens. Good night, Father Timothy."

An indeterminate murmur from the two of them was her only response. Carrying the tray through to the kitchen she set it on the draining board and softly unbolted the back door. A low buzz of conversation from the dining-room told her that for a few moments she would be unobserved. She stepped out into the yard, and lifted the lid of the bin. In the light streaming from the kitchen door she could see the shiny black bags and the square edges of the paler parcel. Nobody had taken it yet. And one day remained before the refuse was collected.

Going back into the kitchen she bolted the door, ran cold water over the cups, switched off the light and went slowly upstairs, feeling as if every bone in her body was aching. It would have been nice to sink into the too soft bed, pull the covers over her head and abdicate from the world for a while, but while she slept someone might come — and if she stayed awake all night she would be fit for nothing in the morning. Unpinning her veil, taking off the ankle-length grey habit which was the Order's concession to modern fashion she ran her fingers through the black hair that curled over her head, pulled on her nightdress and knelt to pray — for the four who were dead, for her own safety, for an end to the killings.

★ ★ ★

"Will you be needing the car this morning, Father?" she greeted Father Stephens as he went into the dining-room where boiled eggs and toast were waiting.

"I'd not planned to use it, Sister. I think that both Father Timothy and I should stay here in case the police call in, though there's nothing more we can tell them. Why do you want the car?"

"I've some business with Mother Dorothy up at the convent."

"Very well." He frowned slightly and then nodded. "I take it your trip up to the convent is essential?"

"Yes, Father. I'll be back in time to

214

make your lunch."

"We shall eat the rest of the vegetable stew," he said, somewhat gloomily.

She had been a few minutes late for mass that morning, she reflected, as she stacked plates and drank her own coffee. Father Stephens had offered it, seeming preoccupied as if his thoughts were being pulled unwillingly in a different direction. Father Timothy had come back from the convent and stalked in without a word. She doubted if he had mentioned this latest killing to Mother Dorothy or any of the sisters. He would probably regard it as idle gossip, she thought with a little grimace. It was no use pretending. She didn't like Father Timothy.

She was still thinking about her unfortunate inability to like certain people when she drove in through the convent gates, slowing to a crawl in case Alice was around.

Nobody seemed to be around. She parked the car and went in through the back door. The kitchen was neat and tidy with no sign of Sister Teresa and no Sister Perpetua popped her freckled face round the door when she went into the passage that led past office-cum-pharmacy and the infirmary.

"Sister Gabrielle? Sister Mary Concepta?" She looked into the infirmary and was confronted by two empty basket chairs.

Walking through into the polished hall she stood in the silence, hearing her own quickening heartbeats. Someone was walking along the upper gallery at the head of the stairs. To the right the door to the storerooms was blocked off. To the left an archway gave on to the narrow corridor that led between the cells. It was from that direction the footsteps came.

"Good morning, Sister Joan." Mother Dorothy paused and looked down.

"Mother Dorothy!" Sister Joan let out her pent-up breath.

"Whom did you expect to see?" the prioress enquired, starting down the stairs.

"I don't know. I couldn't find anybody."

"They are all in chapel. The Friday meditation," Mother Dorothy said. "Surely you haven't forgotten about that already?"

"No, of course not, Mother! I am not thinking straight this morning, that's all. When I couldn't find anybody I couldn't help thinking of the *Marie Celeste*," Sister Joan said.

"You fancied we had all been lifted out of the enclosure by a sea monster, Sister? What an uncomfortably vivid imagination you must have," Mother Dorothy said dryly. "No, they are all meditating in chapel save for Sister Katherine who is suffering from a violent migraine so was persuaded to go and lie down. I slipped out to see if she was feeling better. She is sleeping quietly so we'll leave her to recover as nature intends. Have you come to join in the meditation?"

"No, Mother. I have some further news for you," Sister Joan said.

Mother Dorothy's gaze sharpened as she reached the foot of the staircase but she said only, "You had better come into my parlour. I must rejoin the rest of the community very soon."

Sister Joan went after her superior into the clean, bare parlour. Though the day was cold there was, as usual, no fire in the handsome fireplace where a basket of logs and everlasting flowers filled the hearth space, imparting the only touch of gaiety.

"*Dominus vobiscum*," Mother Dorothy said, seating herself. "What news, Sister?"

"*Et cum spiritu tuo*," Sister Joan responded automatically. "There's been another murder, Mother."

"Another — ?" Mother Dorothy's sandy eyebrows shot up towards her hairline. "You do believe in coming to the point, don't you?" she said dryly. "You had better explain."

"Mrs Fairly, the housekeeper, was killed by an injection of insulin," Sister Joan recapitulated swiftly. "The overdose of Valium — she didn't drink it all. It wasn't suicide, Mother Dorothy. Someone killed her. Her niece was struck on the head while she was on her way here and apparently thrown out of the train. Yesterday I went to meet Miss Potter's friend who was coming down from the north. Father Stephens had invited her to stay at the presbytery. She wasn't on the train. Her body had been found in the boot of a — a car in a garage on the outskirts of town. She'd been hit on the back of the head too — the police think probably by an axe."

"Nobody from the police station has informed me of any of this." Mother Dorothy looked puzzled. "Indeed although the information is very shocking and disturbs me greatly I fail to see why they should. It isn't our direct concern."

"She was found in the boot of the convent car," Sister Joan said.

The prioress drew her breath in sharply and clasped her hands together above the flat, shining surface of the desk.

"Sister Jerome had leave to use the car yesterday," she said. "She had to go further afield than she intended in order to buy the gardening implements that Sister Martha needed. On her way back into town she noticed the clutch wasn't acting correctly and very sensibly turned in at the nearest garage, left it to be repaired and phoned for a taxi back. She dismissed the taxi before reaching the convent gates because she didn't want to spend too much money. She told me all this."

"She didn't say anything to me when I saw her," Sister Joan said.

"Why on earth should she?" Mother Dorothy shot her an icy look. "Sister

Jerome is not obliged to explain her actions to you, Sister. She is in my charge, not yours."

"Yes, Mother Dorothy. I beg pardon." Sister Joan flushed darkly.

"Since you will not be here for general confession tomorrow," Mother Dorothy said, still frowning, "make sure you go to the Sacrament of Penance in the church, Sister. I take it the police will be coming here then?"

"Detective Sergeant Mill said he would drive over later this morning but that I might visit first. I thought Sister Jerome might feel naturally more inclined to talk to a fellow nun than to a police officer."

"Sister Jerome will answer truthfully any questions put to her by the police just as any other member of the public is obliged to do," Mother Dorothy said. "You surely can't imagine that our lay sister is travelling round the country hitting people over the head with an axe? The notion is ludicrous!"

"Mother Dorothy, Sister Jerome doesn't stay in her cell at night." Sister Joan's face had paled now with temper and her blue eyes were stormy. "Sister Teresa and Sister Gabrielle both hear her unbolting the kitchen door and going out. They didn't know whether to mention it to you or not. Sister Gabrielle suggested that I might get into conversation with her, but Sister Jerome isn't the easiest person in the world to have a chat with. And I'm not suggesting that she's killing people but when dreadful things are happening then any sort of behaviour that seems out of the ordinary surely ought to be investigated. I'm sorry if I speak too frankly, Mother, but that's how I feel."

Mother Dorothy was silent for a spell, resting her chin on her clasped hands, her eyes inward and searching.

"You have made your point," she said finally. "I wish you had made it rather more courteously. However you obviously feel strongly, as we all must do, about the recent series of events. I shall talk to Sister Jerome myself, find out if she left the car unattended. She did have a cup of tea while she was in town so it's possible that the unfortunate Miss Hugh was put into the back of the car then. Now, why don't you come with me into chapel and share our meditation. It is on humility and penitence."

"Yes, Mother. Thank you, Mother."

Feeling about two inches high Sister Joan followed meekly into the chapel. The rest of the community, with the exception of Sister Katherine, sat in their accustomed places, their heads bent, veils pulled forward. Custody of the eyes was an important discipline of the regular meditations. She put up her hands to adjust her own veil, raised her eyes in one brief, forbidden glance to the altar and froze.

On the altar, invisible to those who directed their gaze obediently floorwards, placed neatly between two candlesticks beneath the heavy crucifix an axe lay, its cutting edge dyed red by the rays of sunlight struggling through the stained-glass window.

11

MOTHER DOROTHY had seen it too. She stood still, then moved forward, swiftly covering it with one of the altar cloths before turning to the community.

"The meditation is ended," she said firmly. "Go in peace."

Eyes downcast, they rose, blessed themselves, genuflected and filed out. Even Sister Teresa had achieved perfect custody of the eyes, Sister Joan thought guiltily. She herself had never managed it. There were too many interesting things going on all around for her to keep her eyes on the ground.

"It was not on the altar when I left the chapel to tend to Sister Katherine," the prioress said.

"Is the sacristy door unlocked?" Sister Joan asked.

"Yes, Sister. It is unlocked before mass every morning as you know and not closed again until the grand silence.

"And not locked then," Sister Joan murmured.

"The door into the chapel wing from the main hall is locked," Mother Dorothy reminded her. "I will not have the chapel bolted against anyone who may wish to come seeking comfort whether at noon or midnight. We sisters may, in moments of great spiritual need, unlock the inner door ourselves and I'll not deny sanctuary to our lay friends. We are wasting time, Sister. I'll telephone the police immediately."

She genuflected to the altar and went briskly out. Sister Joan, following, saw the familiar squad car circle round and come to a stop before the open doors. Detective Sergeant Mill unfolded his long legs from behind the wheel and came towards them, his glance at Sister Joan one of enquiry.

"Good morning, Detective Sergeant Mill." Mother Dorothy advanced. "Sister Joan has already told me of the most recent events. Something else has happened. Would you please come into the chapel?"

He followed her down the short corridor with no more than a brisk nod in reply. Sister Joan, trailing after them, noticed his swift glance round the chapel. She wondered what he made of it. They had never discussed his personal faith but she guessed that he was probably an agnostic.

"We have been meditating here for the last couple of hours," Mother Dorothy said. "During meditations in Lent we keep strict custody of the eyes. We bow our heads and look only at the floor. We deny ourselves even a glimpse of the altar. We were all here this morning, except for Sister Katherine who is not well. I went out during the meditation to check up on her and met with Sister Joan on my way down. When we came into the chapel there was something laid on the altar. I must explain that as prioress I am permitted to raise my eyes to ensure that everything is in order in the chapel. It was all in order when I left but when I returned — "

With what in anybody less practical might be termed a fine sense of the dramatic she went within the altar rail and lifted the cloth.

"Please don't touch it!" Detective

Sergeant Mill said sharply.

"Fingerprints — I know!" She frowned slightly. "I laid the cloth over it very gently. I doubt if anything has been smeared."

"Will you be able to manage without the chapel for a couple of hours?" he asked. "I know it means a lot to you but I will have to lock it and get the fingerprint team up here."

"It will be a slight inconvenience," she assured him, "but since God doesn't live only in His chapels we shall manage. Do you want me to lock the outside door? There is a key."

"I have to radio the station. I'll go out that way and take the key with me," he said. "Can you lock the other door?"

"If it's absolutely necessary."

"For the moment it is. Where are the sisters now?"

"In their cells writing up the results of their meditation."

"Could you get them together for me? Someone may have seen something."

"Yes, of course." Mother Dorothy frowned more deeply. "I must tell you though that during meditation they would not have raised their eyes. Anyone could have come in without being seen by them or even heard — the carpet is very thick."

"You saw nothing, Sister Joan?" He rounded on her.

"Sister Joan was with me, telling me about Miss Hugh's body having been found. We were standing in the main hall and nobody passed us to go into the chapel."

"Did you enter through the front door, Sister?"

"Through the back door into the kitchen."

"And you were upstairs with Sister Katherine, Mother Dorothy?"

"For no more than a minute or two. When I looked in at her she was sleeping."

"But while Sister Joan was coming in through the kitchen and you were upstairs it would have been possible for someone to walk through the front door?"

"Just barely possible," Mother Dorothy said. "The door was open but if anyone came that way they'd have had very little time in which to cross the hall, go past the visitors' parlour, enter the chapel, put the axe on the altar and then go out again."

"I'll make that call." He ran down the front steps to the car.

"Wait for me in my parlour, Sister," Mother Dorothy said. "I shall call the sisters together."

She paused to lock the inner door leading to the chapel, pocketed the key and went upstairs.

Sister Joan went into the parlour and sat down. She was trembling slightly and there was a sour taste in her mouth. What was happening was bad enough but now it had directly invaded the convent.

The community filed in, Sister Gabrielle grumbling audibly, Sister Katherine looking swollen eyed and pale. Mother Dorothy brought up the rear like a brisk little sheepdog with a docile flock.

"I'm sorry to disturb you all, Sisters." Detective Sergeant Mill had reappeared in the doorway. "I won't keep you longer than I can help. Is everybody here?"

"Sister Hilaria is in the postulancy with Sister Elizabeth and Sister Marie,"

Mother Dorothy said. "They have their own meditations separate from us. Shall I — ?"

"That won't be necessary. The rest of you, apart from Sister Joan who hadn't yet arrived and Sister Katherine — ?" He looked round.

Sister Katherine put up her hand.

"You were sick, Sister?"

"A migraine," Sister Katherine said. "Mother Dorothy told me to go back to my cell and lie down. That was just before we went into meditation."

"At what time did the meditation begin?" He looked at Mother Dorothy.

"At eight-thirty, after we had breakfasted and swept out our cells. It was due to last for two hours."

"But you'd already been in chapel today? For mass?"

"We were all in chapel by five-thirty for an hour's private devotions before Father Timothy arrived to offer mass. He left without taking any coffee with us at — seven-fifteen. We went up to the refectory for breakfast, and returned to chapel at eight-thirty — except for Sister Hilaria who took her charges back to the postulancy and Sister Katherine who looked very unwell. We had been in chapel for about an hour when I decided to slip upstairs and see if Sister Katherine needed anything. That was when Sister Joan arrived."

"During this meditation do you all sit in the same place?" he asked of the company in general.

"We all sat in different places," Sister Gabrielle said with a whinny of amusement. "If you mean did we move from our places I for one didn't. It's hard enough for me to struggle into chapel these days without skipping about once I'm there!"

"I didn't move either," Sister Mary Concepta said.

"Did anybody move?" He looked round the circle of faces.

"I went over to the Lady Altar," Sister David said, putting up her hand and looking terrified. "I didn't lose custody of the eyes, Mother, but that vase of catkins on the floor at the base of Our Blessed Lady's statue looked very untidy so I went over and put some of the branches in more securely."

"Did anybody else move?"

"I went and kissed the steps of the altar," Sister Martha said, adding vaguely, "Left over penance."

"Did anybody see or hear anybody come in or out of the chapel?" He looked round again.

"I am a trifle deaf in the mornings," Sister Mary Concepta said timidly, "so I couldn't have heard."

"Anybody else?"

"We were in a Lenten meditation," Sister Perpetua said impatiently. "That means the most intense and disciplined concentration. We block out all extraneous sights and sounds. At least" — she shot a look towards Sister David — "some of us do."

"May we ask why you wish to know?" Sister Mary Concepta enquired.

"Something was put on the altar while Mother Dorothy was out of the chapel," he said. "None of you went up to the altar?"

"Only to the steps," said Sister Martha.

"Anybody notice anything at all?" There was barely concealed exasperation in his voice.

There was a general shaking of heads.

"Thank you anyway. If anyone did notice anything — anything at all I'll be here for a while or you can tell Mother Dorothy about it in private."

Sister Joan stayed on her stool as the others filed out. Her sick, shaky feelings had been succeeded by a most reprehensible desire to giggle. Obviously Detective Sergeant Mill found it incredible that they could render themselves blind and insensible to what might be going on around them.

"I suppose if someone had been murdered in the middle of meditation," he said, as the door closed behind Sister Teresa, "nobody would have noticed that either!"

"Sister David might have registered the fact that a body was cluttering up the floor," Mother Dorothy said deadpan.

"I believe you, Mother Prioress," he said fervently. "So! Sister Joan has told you about our having found Miss Hugh, the friend who shared a house with Miss Potter, Mrs Fairly's niece?"

"And that she was found in the convent car," Mother Dorothy said. "It is quite

232

illogical of me but that seems to make it worse somehow. I hope that doesn't sound too heartless. Sister Jerome took the car yesterday morning. She had the doctor to see and also several gardening implements to buy and I told her to get herself a cup of coffee while she was in town. The clutch on the car went and she very sensibly took it into the nearest garage and phoned for a taxi."

"I'd like to talk to Sister Jerome if I may."

"Certainly, Detective Sergeant, though I doubt if she can add anything. She'll be in the kitchen. No, Sister, I'll fetch her myself."

She waved Sister Joan back on to her stool and left the room.

"Whose fingerprints would be likely to be in the chapel?" he enquired abruptly.

"Everybody's," Sister Joan said. "Sister David is sacristan — she sees that the vases are kept filled and the candles trimmed and replenished and the vestments ready for when Father comes to offer mass or hear confessions. But all the sisters take turns to clean and polish. All our fingerprints would be there."

"But not on the axe?" His voice was thoughtful.

"Wouldn't the most stupid killer know better than to handle anything without gloves?" she countered.

"Probably but there's always the chance that this one might be arrogant enough to slip up," he said. "Ah, this must be Sister Jerome?"

He was indicating a stool but she remained standing, large feet planted on the polished floor, hands tucked into her sleeves, her person ramrod stiff as if she prepared to face a firing squad.

"I'd just like you to run through what you did yesterday when you went into town," he said in a pleasant conversational tone.

"Nothing against the rule," Sister Jerome said.

"Of course not. I know you had permission to use the car and leave the enclosure. You drove down to town?"

"To register with the new doctor — Dr Phillips. He offered me a free examination so I took it. As a health precaution."

"That's standard practice these days I believe. And after that?"

"I had to wait for more than an hour in the surgery and it was past eleven when I came out."

"And then you did the errands with which you'd been entrusted?"

"I went into a newsagent's to buy manuscript paper for Sister David." She sounded as if the detective was pulling teeth. "Then I had a bill to pay — electricity, and then the gardening clippers and fork to buy."

"Which you couldn't get in town?"

"They were expensive and very heavy. I drove out to the next town and bought what was needed there. I don't see why I'm being asked all these questions."

"Bear with me for a moment more, Sister. On your way home — what time was that?"

"I'm not sure. I wasn't checking the time. The clutch was not engaging properly so I turned in at the garage on the outskirts of town. The man there said he'd fix it and have it back today. I rang for a taxi and came back to the convent."

"With the tools?"

"Yes. Of course. They were needed."

"You took them out of the boot?"

"I put them on the back seat," Sister Jerome said. "What is all this about?"

"Mrs Fairly — the housekeeper at the presbytery — you know that she died?" Mother Dorothy had broken in.

"We offered prayers for her," Sister Jerome said.

"It seems that she didn't after all commit suicide for which we must offer thanks," Mother Dorothy was continuing. "Her niece, Miss Sylvia Potter, was on her way down here to see to her late aunt's effects but she died — she was apparently attacked and thrown from the train and then Miss Potter's friend who was also on her way here after the news had been broken to her — you had better sit down, Sister."

"I would prefer to stand," Sister Jerome said stonily.

"As you please." Mother Dorothy shot a look towards the detective who answered it with a curt nod. "Sister Jerome, the body of Miss Potter's friend was found in the boot of our car. She had been most brutally murdered."

"You're accusing *me*?" The pale face

had gone scarlet, veins stood out on her temples beneath the coif.

"Nobody is accusing anybody yet," Detective Sergeant Mill said.

"I didn't know this woman. I never met her."

"Someone else did meet her though, Sister," he said. "Someone lured her off the train, killed her and put her body in the boot of the car. You say you were an hour in the doctor's surgery."

"An hour waiting and a further half-hour for the examination."

"Where did you leave the car?"

"In the car-park behind the station. There wasn't sufficient room to leave it outside the surgery."

"Can you remember whether or not the boot was locked?"

"I didn't check."

"It never is locked," Mother Dorothy put in. "The key's difficult to turn unless you have the trick of it, so we don't trouble."

"Can you recall exactly where you parked the car?" Detective Sergeant Mill asked.

"Yes. Yes I can." She closed her

eyes briefly for an instant, then opened them again. "At the very far side in the right-hand corner. There's a tunnel there, a kind of walkway connecting the car-park with the station. I left it there."

"You didn't see anybody in the car-park when you were leaving the car or coming back to it?"

"There were some people about. I didn't take much notice."

"And you didn't open the boot?"

"I didn't open the boot." She spoke flatly without emphasis.

"And you didn't see anyone approach the altar during the meditation?"

"I saw nobody. Nobody!" Her voice rose slightly.

"That will do for the moment, Sister." Mother Dorothy had risen. "Would you be good enough to start the soup for lunch? You can write up the results of your meditation later on."

"Yes, Reverend Mother." The stiff figure bent briefly for the blessing and was gone, closing the door firmly behind her.

"She can tell you nothing more."

Mother Dorothy turned to fix Detective Sergeant Mill with a quelling glance. "Sister Jerome came to us only recently with the highest recommendations from our London house. The idea of her being involved in murder is quite out of the question."

"You know anything of her before she entered your Order?" he enquired.

"Our previous lives are of no concern."

"Not to the Order perhaps. However — excuse me a moment. I want to check up." He was gone, striding out rapidly. Through the open door Sister Joan heard his voice raised cheerfully, "The side door's unlocked, Petrie! Wipe your boots before you tramp in, there's a good fellow!"

"Sister Jerome couldn't possibly kill anybody," Mother Dorothy said, looking at Sister Joan. "Believe me, Sister, but if she has such violence in her then I am very wrong in my assessment of human nature."

"I'm not accusing anybody of anything," Sister Joan said.

"One hopes not. Accusations are not our business." Mother Dorothy hesitated, then said unexpectedly, "Since you'll be expected back at the presbytery soon you'd best take your leave. You can go through the kitchen if you've a mind to say goodbye to anyone."

"Mother Dorothy, shouldn't Detective Sergeant Mill be told about the slashing of the oak tree near the postulancy?" Sister Joan asked.

"You really think the information might be relevant?" The prioress thought for a moment, then said, "Very well, I will tell him myself before he leaves."

"There's something more, Mother," Sister Joan said tensely. "The flowers in the front garden of the presbytery were all sliced up and the heads cut off on the morning after I arrived there."

"Not teenage vandalism?" Mother Dorothy shook her head and answered her own question. "No, not that. There is a connection, I feel. I will tell Detective Sergeant Mill. Have you heard whether or not a new housekeeper has been appointed yet?"

"I'm sure that Father Stephens will do his best, Mother."

"One trusts that he will. Very well,

Sister, you may go now. Keep in touch with me, please."

"Yes, Mother." She knelt for the blessing and went out.

A fine thin rain was blurring the windows and blowing through the open front door. Outside another patrol car had arrived and two policemen were conferring in the front seats. The routine of official investigation would be set in motion, threatening to disrupt the conventual routine. She turned and went through into the kitchen. Sister Perpetua was in the infirmary, settling the two old ladies who, judging from Sister Gabrielle's garrulous tones, had been stimulated rather than upset by the arrival of the police. To her relief Sister Teresa wasn't in the kitchen. Presumably she had gone to her cell to write up her meditation. Sister Jerome was chopping vegetables, the big kitchen knife rhythmically moving up and down on the board.

"Sister Jerome." She paused within the door.

"Sister Joan." The other went on chopping the vegetables.

241

"You seem to be keeping the ship afloat while I'm not here," Sister Joan said. "I hope Sister Teresa is helping. I find her a nice girl."

"Sister Teresa does her fair share of the work," Sister Jerome said grudgingly. "As to her being nice or not — surely we are not encouraged to have personal friendships? That, at any rate, has always been my understanding."

"In an ideal world," Sister Joan said. "However one cannot help liking some more than others even if one loves them all equally. It must have been a great shock for you to learn that you probably drove the car round yesterday with a dead body in the boot."

"A very great shock."

Chop, chop, chop went the knife.

"Unless the poor woman was put there later. There isn't any way in which she could have been killed by one of the gardening implements you bought?"

"I had nothing to do with — "

"No, of course not," Sister Joan said quickly. "What I mean is that if you left the things in the back of the car and went to have your coffee before starting home someone might have used one of them — that car doesn't lock very securely at the best of times."

"I didn't buy an axe," Sister Jerome said.

"No, of course not. How did you know it was an axe?"

"You just — the police officer said — " The chopping slowed, stopped.

"No, Sister. Nobody has mentioned an axe. What made you say 'axe'?"

"You think you're very clever, don't you, sister?" The other raised her coifed head, staring at her with hostile dark eyes. "Clever Sister Joan who helps out when a crime is committed! Oh, I know you don't talk about it yourself but others do. We were all told about your exploits in the London house. Such a clever nun, to balance her spiritual life with her amateur sleuthing! And now you're doing it again, aren't you? But not with me. Not with me!"

"Sooner or later they'll take all our fingerprints and match them with any found on the axe handle."

"They'll not find mine there. I wasn't such a fool as to pick it up with my bare hands and — " Sister Jerome stopped dead.

"You wrapped your sleeve around it?" Sister Joan said.

Sister Jerome stood, head flung back, fury gradually dying out of her face, to be replaced by a great weariness.

"It was under my seat in chapel," she said and sat down tiredly on a kitchen chair. "When I knelt down my foot struck against something. I waited until the others were deeply into their meditations before I stooped lower and pulled it out. Even in the dim light I could see the dried blood along the edge. It had been put under my seat deliberately. I didn't know what to do, but then Mother Dorothy got up and left the chapel, so I took it up and went up to the altar and laid it there. I decided that God could deal with it."

"It was used to kill two, possibly three people. Did you know that?"

"I knew nothing — nothing!" Sister Jerome said vehemently. "I guessed it hadn't been employed to slaughter chickens. It was an evil thing an obscene thing. I could feel that, feel that I was going to be blamed, blamed for something I hadn't done, didn't know anything about! I couldn't let that happen. It was very easy. My footsteps can be very light when I choose. Very light! I've had plenty of practice at that."

"Nobody looked up?"

"Nobody did so much as flicker an eyelash," Sister Jerome said. "It took me a few seconds, no more. I returned to my place."

"But you didn't tell Detective Sergeant Mill? Why not?"

"Why should I? He'd only twist it against me! Now I suppose you'll run and tell him like a good little assistant!"

"I'll say nothing unless it becomes absolutely necessary," Sister Joan said. "It would be better if you told him or Mother Dorothy yourself but I'll say nothing. Not for the moment anyway."

She walked past the other, opened the back door, and went into the drizzling rain, not in the least confident that she was doing the right thing.

12

"SISTER JOAN, can you give me a lift back into town?" Detective Sergeant Mill came round the corner as she was getting into the car.

"Did your own car break down suddenly?" she asked warily.

"One of the lads will drive it back when they've finished in the chapel. No, I want to talk to you, Sister."

"I can't tell you anything more at the moment," she began.

"'Can't' or 'won't'? Is there someone else who can?"

"I'm not the keeper of anybody else's conscience."

"Meaning you could if you would?"

"Meaning I would if I could," she corrected. "I'm not trying to keep anything from you, but there are some things that others could tell you more cogently."

"I'll come back and have a quiet chat with Sister Jerome. Thank you,

Sister." He had opened the door and was lowering himself into the passenger seat.

"I haven't told you anything," she said.

"Your face did while I was questioning her. You haven't achieved custody of the eyes yet, have you? She's hiding something, isn't she?"

"Nothing that would materially alter whatever theory you're building up," she said carefully, putting the car into gear. "Sister Jerome will, I think, talk to you herself when she's thought things over."

"That'll have to do for now, I suppose." He shot her a glance as she rounded the corner and headed for the gates. "I'm sure you've been told before that you're a very obstinate woman."

"Occasionally. It's more caution than obstinacy," she defended herself. "I would never withhold material from the police that was vital but I have to use my own judgement sometimes in balancing what is important against what isn't."

"You might try giving me that task."

"I do whenever I can," she protested, "but there are times when my spiritual

247

duty must come first."

"As when Mother Dorothy orders you not to mention that a tree and several bushes were vandalized in the convent grounds?"

"Ah! she's told you then?" Sister Joan allowed herself a small sigh of relief.

"While you were in the kitchen taking your leave of Sister Jerome. The incident ought to have been reported, you know."

"There's so much vandalism these days that Mother Dorothy felt it would only be wasting your time to say anything. And we didn't know then about anybody being killed."

"True, but it still ought to have been noted."

"The flowers in the front garden at the presbytery were all destroyed too. I found them, chopped up and dropped back into the border on my first morning there."

"You didn't mention that either."

"I told Mother Dorothy and advised her to report the damage done to the tree."

"Which she finally did."

"Do you think they are all connected?" she ventured.

"We'll know that when we compare the slashes on the tree with the blade of the axe," he said. "I've got someone checking on that now, but I think we'll find they match."

"Nothing matches," Sister Joan said.

"Some things do and the rest will when we find the connection. There's the damage done to the trees and to the flowers you tell me now — the injuries inflicted on that first victim, the axe blows to Miss Potter and Miss Hugh — so the axe is a factor, a link. We have to find other links and make a chain strong enough to confine a very dangerous person."

"The train down from the north?"

"Two of the victims were travelling down to where another victim had been killed, and the first victim was found by the side of the line probably ambushed in the old tunnel and dragged to the side of the track. There would have been a lot of blood that first time. Anyone catching a train would certainly have been very conspicuous, so we must assume they went somewhere to clean up first. There's a conduit runs along by the line so they could have washed themselves there. The water flows fast so it's unlikely to bear any traces — "

"When will they know who the first victim was?"

"Thanks for saying 'when'," he said dryly. "Oh, they'll do dental checks, identikit portraits based on the shape of the skull etc. The truth is that people do disappear without trace, Sister. Every year hundreds of people walk out of their homes and are never heard of again. Ninety-five per cent of them are runaways trying to leave some intolerable situation behind and make a fresh start, and if we've no reason to think a crime is involved there isn't one single thing we can do about it. The remaining five per cent may be suffering from genuine amnesia, but there's always the odd one who's come to an unfortunate end."

"But relatives and friends report them as missing, don't they?"

"Those who have relatives and friends. Nobody has reported this particular man as a missing person. He may have been a loner, a dropout from normal society. We just don't know."

"What do we know?" she demanded.

"Male, Caucasion, mid-thirties, fairish hair, about five-eight in height, slim build, traces of manual labour on hands — callouses, that kind of thing, no scars or tattoos. The results of the final autopsy should be here very soon. They're letting me have them as soon as they have them. Did Sister Jerome find the axe under her seat?"

"Yes, she — " Sister Joan gripped the wheel and shut her mouth tightly.

"Sorry, Sister." He looked only marginally contrite. "The axe left a faint indentation in the carpet. Is that what she's been hiding?"

"Well, since you figured it out already — " She bit her lip and went on resignedly. "She didn't know what to do. The community was in the middle of a Lenten meditation and she had an axe under her seat! I think she was panicked by the thought that she might be blamed for what's been happening — not that she knew about everything but she certainly knew the tree and the holly bushes had been damaged and she must have feared being blamed for that. So she took the axe and put it on the altar. Nobody looked up or took any notice."

"Did Sister Jerome arrive before or after the tree was vandalized?" Sister Joan frowned, trying to sort events into chronological order.

"After, I think," she said. "No, wait a moment. She arrived in the morning before Father Malone left and Father Timothy got here. I saw Father Malone off at the station, took Father Timothy back to the presbytery, then drove back to the convent. Sister Jerome was here then and shortly afterwards the damage was discovered. I don't think anyone could say when exactly it had been done. Sometime between the start of the grand silence on the previous night and when it was first seen the next morning."

"So Sister Jerome might have gone out earlier and done it herself?"

"She hasn't got a cast-iron alibi you mean. None of us has. Within the rule there is great freedom of thought and a considerable freedom of action. We come together for our prayers and meditations and for meals and recreation but each

252

nun has her own particular duties, most of them solitary."

"Park in the lay-by for a minute or two and run through them for me."

"The duties?" She drew up obediently. "Mother Dorothy is prioress for another three and a half years when we have the elections; Sister David is her secretary and sacristan — she keeps the chapel supplied with candles etcetera, and she's writing a series of short books for children on the lives of the saints. Sister Hilaria has charge of the two postulants, Sister Marie and Sister Elizabeth; and Sister Perpetua is infirmarian. She takes care of Sister Gabrielle and Sister Mary Concepta. Then Sister Katherine deals with all the laundry and makes lace and embroidered vestments for sale and Sister Martha tends the garden and sells some of our produce at market. Oh, and Sister Teresa is helping out as lay sister just before she goes into seclusion before her final profession. And I can't see any of them being mixed up in any of this. Not Sister Jerome either!"

"And you're exiled to the presbytery."

"Only for a week — less than a

week now. Until a new housekeeper is engaged."

"I would feel happier," he said slowly, "if you were back at the convent."

"Nobody is likely to come after me with an axe — though Father Stephens may be tempted if I'm delayed much longer and he has to wait for his lunch."

"Mrs Fairly was killed in the presbytery," he reminded her. "Killed in her own bedroom."

"I've thought about that," she said. "You know the front door is locked and the back door is bolted last thing at night but the presbytery is joined to the church via the sacristy and I don't think anyone troubles to lock the sacristy door and, of course, Father Malone like ourselves with our chapel likes to leave the church door open in case anyone needs spiritual comfort."

"So anyone could get in if they were aware of that." He made an exasperated sound. "Dear God, but when this is over I shall insist on our security officer giving you and the priests a talk on the dangers of modern life. You're all living in the Middle Ages."

"There was violence then too. Look, we can't live in fortresses, Detective Sergeant Mill! At the convent we have Alice — she'll grow up into a splendid guard dog, I'm sure."

"I'll still arrange for that pep talk," he said grimly. "Look, I can walk from here. It's only a couple of minutes. I'll file my report, grab some lunch and then get back to the convent and see if Sister Jerome's ready to talk to me. If she's done nothing then she's no reason to be worried. You'll take care?"

"Yes, of course. Oh, one thing more! I almost forgot — but twenty years ago some vandal damaged the trees in the convent grounds with an axe. It wasn't the convent then, of course. It still belonged to the Tarquin family."

"How do you know this?"

"I'm going through stacks of old newspapers up in the storerooms, cutting out items relating to the immediate area and clipping them together. We're planning on having a big scrapbook just for our own interest."

"Was the culprit caught?"

"I don't know. I only glanced through

the first report of it in the local paper.

"Thank you, Sister. For the lift too. Take care."

He got out of the car and walked off rapidly towards the town centre. So many little pieces, she thought, apparently disconnected and yet connected somewhere. Mrs Fairly had remembered something about Sister Jerome but had died before she could keep her appointment. She had gone up to her room, taken with her the cup of tea with its splash of whisky she indulged in every night, drank some and felt odd, sleepy and disorientated, and then before she could summon help someone had entered her room and injected her with insulin. Insulin of all things! One couldn't just buy that over the counter of the local pharmacy. There was no lock on the bedroom door. Making a mental note to check that the door through into the sacristy was locked later that day, she started the engine again, uttered a small exclamation, and backed on to the moorland track again.

Security. Alice. She'd been up at the convent for quite a considerable period and Alice hadn't put in an appearance. The puppy was always bounding about in the vicinity of the kitchen and the yard, eager to take a walk with anyone who happened to be around. Alice would certainly have come running up, tail wagging, to investigate the police cars, to greet herself. Father Stephens would have to wait a little longer for his lunch. First she'd find out where Alice was.

She turned in at the main gates and parked the car neatly at the side. If she advertised her return she was likely to get bogged down in explanations and questions. She might even cause unnecessary alarm if she started a hue and cry after the puppy. Better to have a wander round before she went into the main house.

She set off at an angle across the grass, skirting the main paths and heading for the postulancy. Alice loved exploring the shrubbery, chasing imaginary foes, stalking birds she never succeeded in catching, burying her bones for future enjoyment.

"Alice! Alice, where are you?" She raised her voice, pausing to disentangle a length of briar from her cloak. "Alice? Here, girl!"

She had pushed her way through the damp shrubbery and reached the perimeter of the tennis court. The rain was still falling lightly but the breeze was mild and the last shining surfaces of the ice had gone.

"Were you looking for Alice, Sister?" Sister Hilaria hove into view, her cloak flung untidily about her shoulders.

"I didn't see her earlier this morning," Sister Joan said.

"Oh, have you been here already today?" Sister Hilaria blinked at her. "I've been in the postulancy with my charges. We had a splendid Lenten meditation. Sister Marie said she had glimpsed a policeman in the grounds, taking photographs of the tree that was damaged. Did Mother Dorothy decide to report it after all? Or has something more serious happened?"

"I'm sure Mother Dorothy will tell you about it," Sister Joan said. The prospect of trying to explain all the ramifications of recent events to the dreamy novice mistress was too daunting.

"You were looking for Alice you said?"

"I haven't seen her this morning," Sister Joan said.

"We had her in the postulancy," Sister Hilaria said. "You know animals are very sensitive to spiritual influences. Mother Dorothy is not inclined to agree with me on that point but I felt that Alice might benefit from our meditation at some level of her nature. It is now generally accepted that domestic animals have simple souls. Probably all animals have souls of some kind. It makes me happy that we are vegetarian though I'm a trifle uneasy about fish even if Our Blessed Lord did catch them — unless those stories are symbolic for the souls of men."

"So Alice is with you?"

"Since our meditation began after breakfast this morning. She lay down and went straight to sleep like a lamb — or perhaps I could say a very good little dog!"

"Then I was worrying about nothing," Sister Joan said, relieved.

"Not that Alice has reached perfection yet by any means," Sister Hilaria said.

"She has great propensity for digging up plants in an effort to get at her bones. And she will insist on presenting whatever she finds to us. Roots, stones, mouldy old biscuits, syringes — "

"Syringes!!"

"One to be exact. She trotted into the meditation with it and laid it at my feet like a gift," Sister Hilaria said, chuckling. "It was covered with dirt and soil."

"Where did she dig it up?" Sister Joan asked sharply.

"I've no idea — somewhere round here, I expect." The novice mistress looked round vaguely. "Certainly close enough for her to hear my voice when I called her."

"What did you do with the syringe?" Sister Joan held her breath.

"Took it away from her of course. The point might have injured her. And it was absolutely filthy, of course too. Sister Elizabeth washed it for me and put it in the cupboard. I meant to ask Sister Perpetua if she ever used a syringe. I didn't think she did but one finds it so difficult to keep up with the speed of events these days."

"If Detective Sergeant Mill comes over to speak to you will you give it to him?"

"Yes, of course I will, Sister," Sister Hilaria said, "but I can't think why he would want to speak to me. I know nothing about the damage to the tree."

"But you do have some knowledge of evil," Sister Joan said.

"And of its coming." Sister Hilaria's somewhat prominent eyes clouded over slightly. "There is a great deal of it about these days. The darkness rises up, I feel. Do you want me to fetch Alice?"

"No, as long as she's all right. I have to get back." Sister Joan nodded and turned away, retracing her footsteps to the driveway where her car waited.

Settling herself behind the wheel she started up the engine and drove fast through the gates out on to the track. Sister Hilaria would completely forget about the syringe within the hour and the syringe was important. Sister Perpetua certainly didn't own one. But someone had buried it near the postulancy. Someone had slashed the tree and destroyed the holly bushes.

She reached the main road again, turned towards the town centre and slammed on her brakes as a policeman on traffic duty shook an admonitory finger at her.

"Sorry, Officer!" She stuck her head out of the window.

"Trying to book yourself an early place in heaven, Sister? Remember the speed limit," he called.

"Sorry." She drove on more carefully, reminding herself that one of her first tasks was to curb her own impulsiveness.

"Sister, you're very late." Father Stephens greeted her coldly as she hurried into the house.

"I'm terribly sorry, Father. I was delayed up at the convent. I'll get your lunch directly. Will you have the warmed-over stew or would you prefer an egg on toast?"

"Anything quick," he said irritably. "I have some sick calls to make this afternoon, and Father Timothy wants to telephone his old seminary and write some letters before he takes confession." Father Stephens went, heavy-footed and disapproving, into the dining-room.

Sister Joan pulled off her cloak and went into the kitchen, grabbing a saucepan and filling it from the tap, putting in four eggs, switching on the cooker and toaster, slicing bread. All actions to be performed automatically while her mind grappled with other things.

"You haven't forgotten the Sacrifice of Penance, Sister?" Father Timothy, coming through the hall, paused at the kitchen door.

"No, Father, I'll be at confession later. Thank you for reminding me," she said bleakly.

No doubt he was saving up a humdinger of a penance especially for her, she mused gloomily.

"I've been hoping we might have some suitable applicants for the post of housekeeper," Father Stephens said, looking at her with rather more favour when she carried in the eggs and toast. "I was a little short with you just now, but it does seem that you seem to be running backwards and forwards between two points and not fully devoting yourself to either of them."

"One cannot serve God and Mammon," she said.

"A singularly inappropriate remark," Father Timothy said with a wintry little smile.

"Sorry, Father." She set down the food and went back into the kitchen to collect the coffee pot, thinking resentfully that she seemed to spend a lot of time these days apologizing to people. Perhaps a good solid bout in the confessional would do her some good.

"Are things going smoothly in the convent?" Father Stephens asked as she poured the two coffees.

"I — think so, Father. I doubt if my absence is much missed. Sister Jerome and Sister Teresa seem to be managing very well between them."

"And you've heard no further developments concerning these recent most unfortunate affairs? Mrs Fairly's death and the two young women?"

"The police take their own time, Father. I daresay we'll be told when something happ — excuse me."

She broke off as the telephone rang in the study.

"Get that, will you, Sister? If it's someone applying for the post I'll be able to interview them later this afternoon," Father Stephens said. "About six."

"Our Lady of — oh, Detective Sergeant Mill!" She broke off as his voice interrupted her at the end of the line.

"Sister Joan? Good, glad I've caught you. We just got the autopsy report on that first body."

"Yes?" Instinctively she had tensed herself.

"Healthy until he was axed to death, non-smoker, liver in good condition, but there's something more. He was a diabetic, Sister. Traces of insulin in the blood and the marks of frequent injections. The pathologist had noticed them before and wondered if he was a junkie. Now we should be able to find out who he was fairly soon. Merely a question of checking all those in the area who get regular supplies of insulin from their local GP and finding out who's gone missing. I'll be in touch."

He had rung off before she could answer him, leaving her clutching the phone.

13

"**I**S everything all right, Sister?" Father Stephens had come into the study and was frowning at her in a concerned fashion as she turned.

"Thank you, yes. That was Detective Sergeant Mill," she said after only a momentary pause. "It may be necessary for me to call in at the police station a little later."

"Does that mean supper will also be delayed?" he enquired.

"No, Father. I'll be back in good time."

"If you must you must, I suppose," he said with somewhat heavy patience.

"I'll see to the clearing-up first," she said placatingly.

There was little point in rushing off to the police station at this moment. The phone call had been a hurried one, probably, she guessed, because Detective Sergeant Mill was on the verge of driving back to the convent to interview Sister

Jerome again. She would look in at the station later in the hope that he might have returned. By then he might have much more to tell her.

Meanwhile there were the dishes to be washed, the carpets to be vacuumed and the surfaces dusted. Mrs Fairly had been dead for such a little while and yet the lack of her careful housewifery was already becoming apparent.

"I'd better get on with my parish visiting then." Father Stephens, mercifully refraining from asking any more questions, turned and went out.

From the dining-room his voice issued cheerfully.

"Would you like to come with me, Father Timothy? We'll be back before you need to go into the confessional. You can ring your seminary later."

"Very well, Father." Father Timothy answered flatly, without intonations of any feelings one way or the other.

"What I would not enjoy very much," Sister Joan muttered under her breath, "would be to be ill and to have Father Timothy visit me on the same day."

Through the back window the square

bulk of the refuse bin partly blocked the light. Now, at least, she had an excuse to go out into the back and wheel it down the side path to the front gate where it would be emptied later.

The front door closed behind the two priests and, waiting a few moments to give them time to reach the garage, she opened the back door and went out.

The empty box she had wrapped up so carefully in brown paper and cellotape had been removed. She dislodged a couple of the black plastic sacks in case it had been pushed further down but there was no sign of it.

She had been correct in her assumption then. The handbag had been roughly wrapped and put in the bin because there hadn't been time to investigate it on the night of Mrs Fairly's murder. Someone had gone there, either after nightfall or during one of her absences from the presbytery to remove it and examine it at leisure.

She wheeled the bin out to the front gate and went back indoors. Whoever had taken the parcel from the bin must know by now that the handbag had been found and a trap set. Sooner or later someone would show his hand.

The rain had stopped and a faint warmth blew on the breeze through the open window of her bedroom. She had made her bed automatically on waking according to conventual habit but she was fairly certain that the two clerics hadn't.

Their rooms were at the other side of the square hallway. Father Stephens had kept his own room, she supposed, noticing a rather touching collection of family photographs on the wall. A cherubic baby in a romper suit held by two proud parents looked as if even then he had been thinking about his Easter sermon; a small boy with his fair hair neatly slicked down held a trophy for something or other; a chubby teenager sat on the arm of a chair with his hand on his father's shoulder; an earnest theological student stood taller than both parents, smiling into the camera. The room was neat even though the bed hadn't been made, a red rug splashing brightness across the floor.

She made the bed, folded the pyjamas,

noting with amusement that Father Stephens favoured a rather jazzy design, and went into the slightly larger room which Father Malone had clearly occupied until recently. The bookcase held his battered collection of old Rider Haggard and John Buchan novels; a pencil sketch of St Patrick exiling the snakes from Ireland hung over the dressing-table, and in a niche between two walls a highly coloured plaster statuette of St Brigid, the 'Mary of the Gael' stood with clasped hands.

The bed had been made, the coverlet smoothed over a curiously flat surface.

Sister Joan stared at it for a few seconds, then abruptly stooped to look under the bed. As she had thought the mattress was stowed there. Father Timothy had elected to sleep on the wooden base. At least he couldn't be accused of preaching penance when he didn't practise it, she thought. His suitcase stood against the wall. She opened the wardrobe door and looked at the black suit and soutane hanging there next to a brown dressing-gown. There was no overt sign of family photographs or any personal possessions. Perhaps he hadn't put them out yet. She closed the door of the wardrobe and bent to the suitcase. It was unlocked and held only a couple of thin towels.

He had had two suitcases, she recalled, one full of paperback books. That was the one she had carried for him and thought very light considering its contents. Presumably he'd put it somewhere else. She took a last look round and went into the room next door. Father Malone had taken his own shabby luggage with him and there were no cases in Father Stephens's room either save a neat weekend case.

The guest bedroom? She went in, looked round and saw Father Stephens's larger case, his initials on the handle, against the wall. Where had Father Timothy put his extra suitcase and the paperback books it had held?

The airing cupboard, the bathroom and the upstairs broom cupboard held nothing that resembled books or suitcase. Going downstairs she looked rapidly in the cupboards there with the same lack of results. There remained the sacristy.

She opened the door, marking with a frown that nobody had troubled to lock it, and looked round at the shelves and cupboards with their consignments of surplices, missals, candles and packets of incense. No suitcase anywhere. Only the richly embroidered copes hanging in the largest cupboard, and on the wall a list of parish notices. The room was still and stuffy, the scent of burnt wax and incense lingering.

"Eureka!" She uttered the word in a tone of triumph as she suddenly saw it, balancing on top of a low cupboard with a pile of altar cloths covering it. There was a stool in the corner. She pulled it into position, climbed onto it, lifted down the cloths, put them on the table, climbed up again and lifted the suitcase down. It was empty. The light weight of it told her that even before she set it down and knelt to the lock.

The case opened easily and she lifted the lid, sitting back on her heels with a disappointed shake of her head as she stared at the empty interior. If it had held books they had been removed. On the handle the initials M. T. were almost rubbed away.

She lifted the case back up to the cupboard and replaced the cloths. There was no reason why Father Timothy shouldn't put one of his cases in the sacristy. It was obviously an old one, shabbier than the one in his room. Brushing dust from her hands she went thoughtfully back into the house. Something was nagging at the back of her mind but she couldn't formulate it into a thought.

On the study table near the telephone a pad held useful telephone numbers, scribbled messages. She went in and sat down to look at it. Father Malone's neat, crabbed hand filled the pages, reminders to get his hair cut and buy toothpaste interspersed with odd numbers jotted down at various times, a list of first communicants and — yes, here it was — Our Lady of Good Hope Seminary and the number next to it.

She lifted the receiver and dialled, wondering when Father Malone would get round to acquiring a more modern instrument. At the other end the ringing had a curious echo, as if it reflected the stone-clad spaces within the seminary. The ringing stopped.

"Our Lady Of Good Hope Seminary. Father Anselm speaking."

It was a cheerful voice with a Lancashire accent.

"This is Sister Joan. I'm calling from Father Malone's parish in — "

"Yes, of course." The voice broke in breezily. "We were in contact with Father Malone recently. What can I do for you, Sister?"

"You've not heard anything of events down here?" she began.

"Events? Father Malone left for his sabbatical, didn't he?"

"Yes. Yes he left. I meant events reported in the newspapers."

"We don't take any newspapers here, Sister. Father Superior reads *The Times* once a week but that's all. Is anything wrong? Father Timothy is well?"

"Yes, he's going to telephone you later. I wondered — did anyone see him get on the train?"

"What an odd question!" Father Anselm said. "Yes, he was escorted to the station according to custom. We like to give our newly ordained priests a good send off. Of course this being Lent only one of us actually accompanied him out of the cloister."

"And came back?"

"Of course he came back, Sister. Why on earth shouldn't he? I fail to see — "

"Please bear with me, Father Anselm," she said quickly. "Could you tell me who went to the station with Father Timothy?"

"Father Philip did. Sister, is something wrong? Father Timothy isn't sick?"

"Is he likely to be?" she countered.

"Not if he continues to take his insulin. He did tell you about that? He is rather shy sometimes about admitting it."

"Yes. We are aware of it. One more question, Father." Without knowing what had suddenly prompted her to enquire she asked, "Have there been any incidences of vandalism at the seminary recently?"

"How odd that you should ask!" Father Anselm said. "Yes, we've had some tools stolen from one of the outhouses as a matter of fact. We don't bother to keep it locked and the wall near it is very low so it would be — easy matter for hooligans to break in."

"Did they vandalize anything?"

"A display of bonsai trees and shrubs on the windowsill. Father Timothy's pet project but happily we were able to keep the news from him since he was leaving the next day. Sister, I've been very patient but I must know why you're asking all these questions."

"I'll telephone you, or Father will. Thank you, Father Anselm."

She replaced the receiver and rested her chin on her hands while she pondered what she had heard. Father Timothy was a diabetic: the body found at the side of the railway track had been full of insulin — a diabetic too or killed in the same manner as Mrs Fairly with the savage axe attack merely designed to draw attention from the real cause of death? Father Timothy had been seen off at the station, and had duly arrived in Bodmin. She ought to have asked if he'd come down on the overnight train.

There was still the vacuuming to do. She rose and went to get the vacuum cleaner, thankful that for once she had something practical to do with her hands while her mind ranged over various possibilities.

What was it that she had heard about Father Timothy before his arrival? The trouble was that she hadn't taken much notice since at that stage she hadn't known she'd be coming down to help out at the presbytery. He was newly ordained, a late vocation which fitted Father Timothy who showed all the symptoms of over-enthusiasm which newly fledged clerics sometimes displayed and he was nearer forty than thirty. He hadn't mentioned his diabetes but as Father Anselm had said he was somewhat shy about it. So shy that she had seen no trace of needles or syringe in his room. She reminded herself that she hadn't gone poking through the drawers of the dresser. There was something else, something she'd been told, something she'd heard — she switched off the vacuum cleaner and unplugged it. Whatever it was would come to her in due course.

It was time to share her knowledge with Detective Sergeant Mill. She went back into the study and lifted the telephone again.

"You just caught me, Sister." His voice sounded pleased. "I only now walked in. What can I do for you?"

"Could you meet me for a cup of coffee?" she enquired.

"Yes, of course. At the cafe? I can be there in a couple of minutes."

"I'll be there in five. Thank you." She put down the receiver and went to get her cloak.

Outside the last puddles were drying in a belated sun and the surfaces of cobbles and paving stones still faintly gleaming. She walked briskly down the street, crossed and turned the corner into the main street. It would have been possible for her to walk into the police station, of course, but some natural caution had dictated another course.

He had tactfully installed himself at a table in the corner and signalled the waitress for a second cup of coffee as Sister Joan entered.

"You've something to tell me, Sister?" He waited until she had taken her first sip, then leaned forward attentively, his voice low.

"Yes, I believe so. Did you speak to Sister Jerome?"

"And to Sister Hilaria." He cocked an eyebrow at her. "You could have told me yourself, you know."

"I went back to the convent to check on Alice's whereabouts and met Sister Hilaria. She mentioned that Alice had dug up a syringe."

"Which she promptly handed over to one of the novices to wash! Didn't it occur to her to report it?"

"Why should she?" Sister Joan protested. "All that Sister Hilaria knows is that a tree and some bushes were vandalized and that Mrs Fairly, whom she didn't know, died. Mother Prioress doesn't fill her time with long accounts of murders for the rest of the community."

"Sorry, Sister." He grinned, holding up a shielding hand. "You're right. Sister Hilaria keeps her thoughts on higher matters, and in any case the tree wasn't attacked by a syringe. She came over to the main house with the syringe. We rushed it to the lab, but when a nun cleans something she cleans it thoroughly. It could have been used to give an injection of insulin. I've a couple of lads up by the tennis court digging at the moment to see what else is waiting to be dug up."

"And you spoke to Sister Jerome?"

"With immense care since she seems to be terrified of police officers — not that I read anything into that. Many innocent people feel an uneasy frisson of guilt when a member of the force hovers into view. She found the axe under her seat, feared that she might be blamed for damaging the tree and put it on the altar while the other nuns were deep in meditation. Her prints were on the handle — very blurred since she'd wrapped the thing in the skirt of her habit when she picked it up. She's a strong woman, by the way, to manage it with one hand. That's quite a weight."

"Yes." Sister Joan nodded.

"Your turn, Sister. You said you had something to tell me." He was looking at her keenly.

"I suppose the poor man who was found up north by the railway track hasn't been identified yet?"

He shook his head. "We've pieced together a reasonably good description of him from forensic evidence, but there's no official report of anyone of that description missing that's been officially logged."

"You said over the telephone that insulin was found. Was he killed by insulin?"

He shook his head again. "No. As far as they can determine the first blow on the back of the head killed him. The other injuries were inflicted in a kind of frenzy. They've found traces of blood matching his in the tunnel by the by. The insulin had been injected before his death and the needle marks show he was an habitual user. It'll take some time to check through medical records but eventually we'll get a result.

"I can save you the trouble," Sister Joan said tensely. "Our new priest, Father Matthew Timothy, is a diabetic. I checked with the seminary."

"But Father Timothy's down here," Detective Sergeant Mill said blankly.

"I thought he might have been the

dead man," she confessed. "Nobody from the seminary would have missed him because he'd officially left anyway, and since they don't get a popular newspaper they wouldn't know about the murder either."

"And?"

"Father Timothy was escorted to the station by Father Philip, another priest at the seminary," she said, "so he can't be the dead man. But there's something else: Father Anselm to whom I spoke said that some tools had been stolen from a garden shed in the seminary grounds the night before Father Timothy left and some bonsai trees and plants were destroyed at the same time. Father Timothy had been cultivating them."

"Has he mentioned this?" Detective Sergeant Mill asked sharply.

"He left before anyone told him about it."

"Two diabetics?" He bit his lip thoughtfully. "It's a common condition but even so — the arm of coincidence does seem to be getting rather long, doesn't it? How did you manage to get all this information? This Father Anselm?"

"I asked a few questions."

"Evidently the right ones. Is there anything else, Sister?"

She hesitated, stirring her coffee round and round, watching the tiny bubbles rise to the surface and break.

"Mrs Fairly's handbag was missing," she said at last.

"It wasn't among her belongings?"

"I packed everything away ready for when her niece came. I just didn't think of a handbag at the time," she confessed. "It's so long since I carried one myself. I only thought of it later."

"You say it was missing? I take it that you've found it?"

"In the refuse bin," Sister Joan said.

Detective Sergeant Mill sat up straighter.

"What made you look there?" he demanded.

"I didn't. I was putting out a refuse sack into the big bin and there was this square brown paper parcel tucked in among the bags. The size and shape were right so I took it out and the handbag was inside. Whoever killed her needed to examine that handbag for some reason but perhaps there wasn't time so they made a parcel and put it in the bin meaning to collect it later. The refuse isn't collected until later today."

"Where's the handbag now?"

"I gave it to Padraic Lee to look after for me."

"Why not bring it to the police?"

"Because finding it gave me an idea as to a way I might find out who'd put it in the bin."

"How? You haven't been mounting guard over it!"

"I put an empty box in the refuse bin, wrapped up in brown paper," she said. "I thought it might force whoever found it to reveal themselves."

"Of all the stupid, amateur — " He scowled at her. "Sister Joan, didn't it enter your head that you were putting yourself in very grave danger? Not to mention Father Stephens and Father Timothy who might equally well have found it originally?"

"I had to think of something on the spur of the moment so I came up with that," she said, flushing, "and if you're going to grumble that I've left it a bit late to tell you what I did your own reaction is the answer. I knew that you'd disapprove."

"Well, at least you've told me now." He was clearly trying to control his irritation. "Sister, we have the resources to deal with something like this. There might have been prints on the handbag. You had no business to suppress evidence."

"I'm sorry." She fiddled with her coffee spoon.

"We'll get on to it now. I don't suppose much harm has been done." He was preparing to rise but she broke in.

"It's gone."

"What!" He sat down again.

"I looked in the bin today after lunch when I wheeled it round to the front ready for collection and it's gone — the parcel I put in. Someone took it."

"And by now will know that the empty box was substituted for the handbag. Sister, hasn't it entered your head that you've put yourself in some danger?"

"Isn't that one way to bring the killer into the open?" she argued.

"An exceedingly reckless way — or are you under the impression that your habit protects you? You've set yourself up at the very least as bait."

"Not exactly," she said slowly. "If they guess I took it, and it's reasonable to suppose that they might, they're not going to do anything to me until they find out where I've hidden the original handbag. I'm positive they were searching in it for something."

"I'd better drive out to the Romany camp and take charge of it," he said. "Sister, it would be wiser for you to leave the presbytery and return to the convent immediately. I can leave a couple of men there to patrol."

"Then I've gone to a lot of trouble for nothing," she said coldly.

For an instant their glances met and locked. Then Detective Sergeant Mill gave an unwilling grin.

"If it was anyone except you, Sister — you presume on the respect I have for your abilities you know. All right! Stay at the presbytery for the moment. The first intimation you have that something is wrong, that someone is getting ready to accost you and you don't wait around to find out. You ring me immediately. Have I your word on that?"

"Yes, of course," she said promptly.

"So where does that leave us?" He sat down again, ticking off items rapidly on his fingers.

"Three instances of mindless vandalism," she contributed. "The bonsai trees at the seminary, the tree at the convent and the flowers in the presbytery garden. The insulin."

"A diabetic priest and a dead body of a diabetic, a woman killed by insulin injection and an empty syringe dug up at the convent," he nodded. "A handbag that was taken, stuffed into the refuse bin to be examined later. Those are the common factors but what we have to sort out is the common link."

"You haven't mentioned the murders," she said.

"Oh, they're the obvious link," he agreed. "All apparently motiveless which would suggest a random killer, a maniac, but committed in different ways — one brutally mutilated, another injected with insulin after a cold-blooded attempt to mislead us into thinking it suicide, a young woman hit over the head while travelling by train and thrown out and her friend killed by a similar blow after she arrived presumably, since her body was found stuffed into the boot of the car that Sister Jerome was using. The last three victims are connected by very slender threads. Sylvia Potter was Mrs Fairly's niece and she shared a house with her fellow schoolteacher, Miss Hugh. Why did they all become victims and what the devil do any of them have to do with a man who was almost certainly engaged in manual labour at some time and who regularly took insulin for his diabetic condition?"

"I don't know," Sister Joan said. "I've thought about it until I feel dizzy."

"Don't come up with any more bright ideas, Sister," he begged, his grin down curving. "Are they looking for a new housekeeper at the presbytery?"

"Yes, of course, but it takes a little time to find the right person."

"And meanwhile you're stuck there instead of being safely tucked up in your convent where you ought to be. I'm going to have to interview Father Stephens and Father Timothy rather thoroughly. They may have seen or heard something that throws light on everything. They may know something important without being conscious that they know it. When are they likely to be in?"

"They're out sick visiting this afternoon and then Father Stephens is coming back to interview prospective housekeepers and Father Timothy is hearing confessions."

"And where will you be?"

"In the confessional," she said feelingly. "Collecting a load of penance to say if I'm any judge of character."

"I'll do my best to get along later. You'll take care, Sister?"

"Yes," Sister Joan said gravely. "Yes, I'll take very great care."

14

THE presbytery was still empty when she let herself in with her key. The rest of the vegetable stew sat sadly in the big pan on the cooker. She looked at it with marked distaste. It was a sin to waste food but both Father Stephens and Father Timothy deserved something a bit more appetizing when they got in. There was some pasta in the cupboard. She'd cook that, heat the vegetables with a good big handful of parmesan cheese and use it as a sauce. Meanwhile she had a little time left in which to collect her thoughts together on paper. When she wrote things down they often assumed a clarity they didn't have when they were tossing about in her head.

She found pad and paper in the kitchen drawer and sat down at the table. Where to begin? Everything was happening so quickly that the sequence of events was becoming blurred. First had been the murder of the unknown, and apparently unmissed diabetic. He must have been killed at about the same time that Father Timothy was being escorted to the station. She wrote down the two events and stared at them, tapping the end of the pen against her teeth.

Whoever had committed that first murder had gone to considerable trouble to render his victim unidentifiable. Whoever had committed that first murder had obviously been splashed with blood. Yet by the time the nuns had entered the grand silence at 9.30 that same night he had been near the convent, near enough to damage the tree and the holly bushes. He had cut it fine, she mused, and tapped her teeth again.

Early that morning Father Malone had left on his sabbatical and Father Timothy had arrived with his two suitcases. One of them stood in his bedroom, the other was in the sacristy and so far she hadn't seen any of the paperback books which it had contained. Later that day had come the telephone call from Mrs Fairly, requesting a meeting, intimating she knew something about Sister Jerome, the new lay sister.

And Sister Jerome had arrived at the convent that same morning that Father Timothy had come. No, she hadn't! She had turned up the day before, striding through the gates with her unfriendly manner. Sister Joan crossed out what she'd written and started again.

1st Sister Jerome arrives.
2nd Father Malone leaves.
3rd Father Timothy arrives. I show him to presbytery.
4th Mrs Fairly telephones me to ask for a meeting in the café.
5th Mrs Fairly's body is found. Believed suicide.
(First victim already discovered up north.)
6th Sylvia Potter killed on way here and thrown from train.
7th Stephanie Hugh killed after arriving here.
Queries.
Why was that first man rendered unidentifiable?
What did Mrs Fairly know about Sister Jerome?
Why was the handbag hidden away?

To be searched later? If so, for what?

Why did Father Timothy have two suitcases? Books? Where are these books?

Is the syringe Alice dug up the one that was used to kill Mrs Fairly?

Is the axe that Sister Jerome put on the altar the murder weapon? Did she really find it beneath her seat? And why is she so certain that she'd be blamed?

Finally she wrote,

Do I know something without knowing that I know it?

A voice from the doorway made her start violently.

"Something smells very tasty," Father Stephens said.

"I'll have it ready for you in five minutes, Father." She hastily closed the pad and rose, thrusting it back into the drawer. "Will Father Timothy be in?"

"He went straight into church to prepare for the confessional." Father

Stephens sighed slightly.

"He's very conscientious, isn't he?" Sister Joan said neutrally.

"As we all must be," Father Stephens said. "Father Timothy never leaves one item of his duties skimped or neglected. It is merely that one doesn't wish to be constantly reminded of duties to be done. Father Malone is far less — censorious."

He brought the last word out reluctantly and immediately looked embarrassed.

"Father Timothy is newly ordained and probably still under the illusion that he's all set for a life of sanctity," Sister Joan said.

Father Stephens gave a choking laugh and looked embarrassed again.

"One really ought not to be too critical," he said apologetically. "The problem is that Father Timothy hasn't yet acquired the right manner when dealing with people. He is quite alone in the world and seems to have no friends or hobbies. One must excuse him a great deal, Sister."

"I suppose." Sister Joan stirred more cheese and a large pat of butter into the sauce and looked rather doubtfully at the pasta. "*Al dente* is the way it's supposed to be but I'm not sure how *al dente* that is."

"I'll just wash my hands." Father Stephens, regaining his mantle of cool superiority, went on upstairs.

"If you've everything you need, Father," Sister Joan said, carrying in the supper, "I'd better go to confession. Oh, nobody called about the post of housekeeper but I had to go out for a short while earlier so it's possible that somebody rang and decided to call in later on the off chance you'd be here."

"No further news on these recent dreadful events?" He looked up at her as he took his seat.

"Nothing to speak of, Father. The police are still investigating. Oh, Detective Sergeant Mill will be calling here sometime. He didn't say when."

"I doubt if I can help him further," Father Stephens said. "Mrs Fairly is to be buried tomorrow. I still wonder if I ought not to get in touch with Father Malone but there really is nothing he can do and it would be a great pity to spoil his pilgrimage."

"I think you're right, Father. If you'll excuse me I'll leave you for now." Going out, she took her cloak from the hallstand and slipped it over her shoulders.

The church was dimly illumined by the perpetual lamp which glowed redly by the altar and by candles lit earlier by those parishioners who had the habit of popping in for a few minutes while out shopping. It would be a pity if the church had to be locked save for services, she thought, because of any fear of vandalism. But, of course, it wasn't mindless vandalism that lay behind the destruction of trees and flowers. It had been something more, something more subtle, more dangerous.

She had entered via the sacristy and closed the door softly behind her as she stood near the altar. Two women were saying their penances nearby and a third left the confessional as Sister Joan genuflected and walked down the aisle to the back of the church.

Usually she spent at least an hour thinking about her faults before she went to confess them, but today if she was to get the rest of the pasta cooked, the sauce warmed over again, fresh coffee brewed, the dishes washed and the parlour ready for any prospective housekeepers who might turn up, there simply wasn't time. The calm and regular routine of the enclosure which made ample time for both the spiritual and the practical really did have a great deal to recommend it.

She stepped into the penitent's half of the confessional, closed the door, and knelt on the hassock by the close-meshed grille. She could discern the austere profile of Father Timothy by the faint light from the other partition.

"Father, forgive me because I have sinned. It is ten days since my last confession." Whispering the customary opening she wondered just how anonymous she now was. Few lay people confessed more than once a month and many saved everything up for the obligatory Easter confession.

"Pray God you make a good confession," came the whispered reply.

"I have harboured uncharitable thoughts," she began, wondering if the day would ever dawn when she didn't have that to confess. "I have spoken too sharply on occasion. I have hurried through my prayers instead of taking time to compose myself. I have sometimes spoken when I ought to have kept silent and kept silent when it was my duty to speak. I have sometimes followed my own will out of obstinacy and pride."

"Your sins are very grave," the voice whispered. "They shock me very much."

But they ought not to shock you, she thought irritably. Priests weren't there in the confessional to make personal judgements. They were no more than a bridge between penitent and Creator.

"Is there anything else on your conscience?" The voice came again.

"I've finished my confession, Father," she whispered firmly.

"Then, for your penance, say one hundred Hail Marys and keep all-night vigil before the altar. Make a good Act of Contrition. *Te absolvo* — "

The words of the confiteor had flown right out of her head. She knelt, half hearing the words of absolution, the severity of the penance having almost taken her breath away.

"Go in peace to love and serve the

Lord and carefully avoid the occasions of sin." Rising, she backed out, opening the door with relief and feeling the rush of cool air. It was going to be rough luck on anyone who had adultery, falsehoods or theft to get off their consciences, she thought. They'd be on their knees until Christmas.

There certainly wasn't time to start her penance now. She'd have to return later and get the prayers said while she was undertaking her vigil.

She genuflected and went back through the sacristy. The shabby case still protruded its corners from beneath the altar cloths on top of the cupboard.

"You weren't long, Sister." Father Stephens looked up from his coffee as she went into the dining-room.

"I haven't said my penance yet."

"Five Hail Marys ought not to take you too long," he said with faint surprise. For Father Stephens the recitation of five Hail Marys was his standard ration of penance. Sister Joan made no comment. To have informed him of her own penance would have felt like tale bearing.

She had finished her own supper and

cleared away when Father Timothy came through from the sacristy. He looked not tired but elated as if hearing the long lists of other people's sins had engendered in him a curious satisfaction.

"Just bread and a glass of milk for me, Sister." He put his sandy head in at the kitchen door. "I make a habit of fasting on Fridays. It is not, I understand, a great feature of the rule up at your convent."

"We eat less during Lent," Sister Joan told him. "And on Good Friday we have only bread and water, but our rule doesn't encourage rigorous abstinence."

"A pity!" he said coldly. "Your Order would be the better for it."

"If you think so, Father." She spoke equally coldly as he went on into the dining-room.

One respected the office of a priest at all times, she reminded herself, but being a cleric didn't automatically turn a man into a pleasant person. No doubt several of the saints had been rather difficult to live with.

When the front doorbell rang she went to answer it just ahead of Father Stephens who was coming out of the study.

"Good evening, Sister Joan." Detective Sergeant Mill had the collar of his raincoat turned up and looked as if he were auditioning for a role in a gangster movie. "I'm sorry to disturb you, Father Stephens, but I did want a few words."

"Yes, of course. Sister, make some coffee, will you?" Father Stephens turned towards the parlour.

"No coffee, thank you, Sister. I'd like you to join us if you will. Is Father Timothy available?"

"He's just about to have his supper," Father Stephens said.

"Food ought not to interfere with one's duty." Father Timothy had appeared at the dining-room door. "If you wish to speak to me — ?"

"Detective Sergeant Mill, Father Timothy. You're here to stand in for Father Malone while he's away?"

"Yes. This is my first parish," Father Timothy said. "I am, of course, aware of some very unfortunate things having occurred here. It casts a cloud."

"Which we hope to dispel. The parlour would be fine, Sister." He ushered her

301

ahead of him, the others following. "This is an informal meeting. A few odds and ends to clear up. As you know Mrs Fairly didn't commit suicide."

"Thank God," Father Stephens said quietly. "I am not saying that murder is a nice business but self-slaughter is so infinitely sad, and had it been suicide I would always have felt, as would Father Malone, that we had failed her in some way."

"At least you need not have blamed yourself, Father Timothy, since you had only just met her," Detective Sergeant Mill said.

"She seemed a very worthy woman," Father Timothy said. "Not that I have much experience of housekeepers as yet, this being my first curacy."

"She always made Father Malone and myself very comfortable," Father Stephens said.

"And you, Sister? You knew her slightly too?" The detective glanced at her.

"I met her briefly on two or three occasions." Sister Joan wondered where all this was leading them.

"You've no knowledge of any enemies

she might have had, Father Stephens?"

"I would have sworn that she had none," he said promptly. "She was a widow, no children, no close family beyond her niece, Sylvia Potter, who lives — lived I ought to say — some considerable distance away."

"Further north, yes." Detective Sergeant Mill nodded absently. "A schoolteacher, not yet thirty years old, shared a house with a fellow teacher, a Miss Stephanie Hugh. Both were well liked, respectable, had boyfriends but nothing serious — there hasn't been an enemy of either of them crawl out of the woodwork so far."

"I still think it must have been a maniac," Father Stephens said.

"These two young women seem to have been specifically followed and targeted," Detective Sergeant Mill said. "It really is beyond the bounds of coincidence that a maniac killing on impulse should light upon three people so closely connected. No, there was a specific motive for killing the three of them. We shall unravel it in due course I've no doubt. You're a diabetic, Father Timothy?"

"Yes I am." If Father Timothy felt any surprise at the abrupt change of subject he gave no sign.

"I didn't know that!" Father Stephens exclaimed.

"It isn't something I choose to advertise," Father Timothy said. "The condition doesn't interfere with the work I do. It's under control at all times."

"You take insulin injections to stabilize your blood sugar levels?"

"I used to but recent advances in treatment enable me to control it through diet alone. Most diabetics these days are extremely healthy."

"What did you do with your syringe when your style of treatment changed?"

"I gave it to Father Superior to be returned to the doctor the next time he visited the seminary. The doctor left it with me together with a supply of insulin in case the diet didn't work properly, and I required an injection in a hurry."

"And the doctor's name?"

"Er — Banning, I think. Yes, Banning. He came very seldom. I cannot see how — oh, yes I do see. You think that the syringe I once had might have been used to — but really, Detective Sergeant, I cannot for one moment believe that Father Superior — there are thousands of diabetics in the country."

"One of them ended up dead on the northern line," Detective Sergeant Mill said.

There was an instant's pause. Then Father Stephens said in a bewildered tone, "Are you referring to that most disturbing headline that was in the newspaper? The unidentified man beaten to death and left at the side of the track?"

"There does seem to be some connection. I don't suppose you saw anyone who was acting in a suspicious manner on your way to the station when you were setting out here?"

Father Timothy shook his head.

"I was with Father Philip," he said. "We were talking about various matters — my impending journey mainly. I doubt if either of us would have noticed anyone in particular."

"Surely it would have been dark anyway," Sister Joan said. "You came down on the overnight train, didn't you?"

"The late afternoon train. I broke my journey in London. The train got in there at just before midnight. I had a very light meal and took an underground train to the station, and caught the early train down into Cornwall. You saw me there, Sister."

"In the waiting-room, yes."

"I saw that Father Malone was receiving quite a send-off from his parishioners and I'd no wish to divert attention from him so I slipped into the waiting-room until the train had left. Sister Joan was kind enough to direct me here to the presbytery."

"That seems clear enough." Detective Sergeant Mill smiled and nodded. "Can I take it that since then you and Father Stephens can account for your time satisfactorily?"

There was another silence. Then Father Stephens said, "Surely you don't think that either of us could possibly have had anything to do with any of this? It's ludicrous!"

"We were both sleeping in the presbytery on the night Mrs Fairly died," Father Timothy said uneasily.

"The sacristy door was open as was the church door," Father Stephens reminded him.

"Meaning someone from outside could have gained access. That's probably it then." Detective Sergeant Mill nodded again. "By the way, her handbag was stolen. Someone wrapped it up roughly in brown paper and sticky tape and put it in the refuse bin. One of the lads found it and had the bright idea of substituting an empty box for it. We've been watching the presbytery on and off for the last couple of days."

"Did you obtain any results?" Father Stephens asked.

"Unfortunately we didn't. Someone was too quick for us and took the substitute parcel when we were engaged elsewhere. Shortage of manpower limits our effectiveness."

"Why would someone put her handbag in the bin?" Father Timothy asked.

"Probably afraid his fingerprints might be on it. He may have picked it up while he was in Mrs Fairly's room, looked inside and then panicked. I take it that neither of you heard anything suspicious during the night?"

"Nothing at all." Father Stephens shook his head. "Mrs Fairly brought our supper and afterwards we — that is Father Timothy and I — went for a short walk. It was a chilly evening."

"Yes indeed. Quite a storm threatening. It never actually broke though," Father Timothy said.

"I insisted Father Timothy went back for his coat and muffler," Father Stephens supplied.

"You didn't see anyone hanging round the presbytery?"

"No, I merely took down my coat and muffler from the hallstand, called to Mrs Fairly that it was only me — she was in the kitchen washing-up, I believe — and rejoined Father Stephens. We had our stroll, returned to the presbytery and I went straight up to my room. I said my prayers and went to sleep almost immediately."

"I came upstairs shortly afterwards too, called goodnight to Mrs Fairly and went into my room."

"And slept like a baby too, I suppose?"

"I'm afraid so, Detective Sergeant."

"And Sister Joan hadn't even arrived, since Mrs Fairly was still alive and housekeeper here. It's a puzzle all right."

"Is there anything else?" Father Stephens enquired as the detective rose.

"Not for the moment. Pity we bungled the surveillance on the refuse bin. I'll see myself out. Goodnight."

And why, thought Sister Joan, watching his retreating back, did he lie about the handbag? To protect me? To bait the trap further?

Something had been said earlier, something that hovered at the back of her mind but refused to come into conscious memory. Something important, something that proved a lie. She wished she could recall what it was.

15

"ONE hopes this terrible business will soon be cleared up," Father Stephens said, sending a worried frown after the closed door. "It makes one lose faith in the goodness of human nature."

"You would call human nature good, Father?" Father Timothy spoke with sudden and biting harshness. "I call it evil and depraved. Even apparent kindness is only self-interest and conceit. I learned that many years ago when I was a boy. Oh, if you think there is anything good in mankind then you are deluded. Deluded!"

"Father Timothy, one must have a sense of proportion," Father Stephens began, but the other had turned, fumbling at the handle of the presbytery door, his eyes blazing coldly in his set face.

"I shall take a short walk," he said, "and then pray in the church for an hour or two. I shall forego my supper in reparation for sin."

He was gone, the door closing with a sharp click behind him. Father Stephens gave an embarrassed cough and looked helplessly at Sister Joan.

"Highly strung," he said vaguely. "One's time in the seminary can lead to a certain inward dwelling quality which makes early parish work difficult. You may clear away, Sister, and lock up but you'd better leave the sacristy door unlocked so that Father Timothy can get in. I'm not sure if he has his key. I gave him Father Malone's for use while he's here. Sister, you must forgive me for saying this if it sounds uncharitable but I wish they had provided us with somebody else from the seminary."

"I know exactly what you mean, Father Stephens," she said feelingly and went into the dining-room to clear away.

Something had been said, something that didn't tie in with something else that had been said — something so trivial that she couldn't bring it to mind. She could only feel it waiting to come into the light of conscious memory.

Perhaps Detective Sergeant Mill was

waiting about outside in the expectation of contriving to have a private word with her. The questions he had asked during his recent brief visit had struck her as fairly pointless, questions that Constable Petrie could equally well have asked while carrying out routine investigations. He had come, she decided, in order to plant the story of the police having found Mrs Fairly's handbag, to divert attention from her own activities. Had he driven up to the convent and planted the same falsehood there? If she rang Sister Perpetua — she glanced at her watch and frowned. They would be in recreation now. Only Sister Teresa and Sister Jerome would be in the kitchen, and she could hardly start asking Sister Jerome since the lay sister might be the one Detective Sergeant Mill was trying to mislead.

She still had her penance to do. Or was that part of it all too? The vigil in the empty church could become a trap, she thought nervously. She went back into the kitchen, fished out the few notes she had made from the drawer and sat down with the pad on her knee.

Father Timothy was a diabetic. Father Timothy had been escorted to the station by a Father Philip. Father Timothy had arrived with two suitcases. Father Philip had escorted him to the station, but not to catch the overnight train. Yet Father Timothy hadn't arrived until just after Father Malone had left. Father Malone had mentioned something about that, something dropped into the brief farewell chat he had had with the community before he left on his sabbatical. Father Timothy had offered mass at the convent and left without taking coffee with the sisters.

She thrust the pad back into the drawer. There was a thick exercise book beneath it with *Household Accounts* printed on a white label on the cover. Father Stephens had mentioned something about Mrs Fairly keeping regular accounts. Sister Joan drew it out and opened it, rifling through the conscientiously written lists of groceries with prices neatly marked and added at the sides. Mrs Fairly had taken pride in her efficiency. There was a newspaper cutting slipped into the most recent page, its edges jagged where it had been torn out. An old cutting, its print yellowish. For a moment she fancied it was the cutting she had seen and put with her pile ready for the scrap book but she had cut hers out neatly with scissors. This had been torn out and folded small as if it had been kept for a long time.

Local housewife gives Evidence, the headline read.

Underneath the accompanying photograph was the report:

Mrs Anne Fairly yesterday identified the teenager accused of vandalizing the woods near the Tarquin estate as John Moore, of Bodmin. Moore who has a history of mental illness was arrested and appeared in an identity parade. It is understood that he will be sent for trial at the Quarter Sessions. Moore, has held only casual labouring jobs since being discharged from the Home for Disturbed Children three years ago. It is expected that if found guilty he will be referred for treatment.

And there was the photograph of a younger Mrs Fairly, standing outside the police station, and looking rather pleased at her sudden prominence.

Even twenty years before identity parades had been discreet affairs, but Anne Fairly had been pleased with her own public spirited action. She had allowed her name to be used, had posed smilingly for the local Press photographer. And twenty years later — Sister Joan put the cutting back into the Accounts book and returned everything to the drawer. From the bottom of the stairs Father Stephens called a goodnight. She heard her own voice answering him and the sound of his footsteps going up the stairs.

It was time, she thought, to begin her penance.

The church was dim and quiet. There was a comforting glow coming from the red sanctuary lamp and a scant half-dozen candles guttering on their spikes before the Lady Altar. At the back of the church the bulk of the confessional was black against the light stone of the baptismal font. She closed the sacristy door and stood in the deep shadow at the side of the High Altar, waiting.

The main door opened slowly and the greyish light of evening bisected the dark. The figure stood for a moment, then came in, letting the door swing back, one hand reaching into the holy water stoup for the ritual blessing. Rising from a genuflection, Father Timothy began to walk slowly down the main aisle.

"Were you looking for me, Father?" Sister Joan asked.

He had stopped short, his indrawn breath clearly audible in the silence. Then he said in his normally dry, stiff manner, "I came here to pray, Sister. You are here to do your penance, I assume?"

"No, I'm not." She had clasped her hands tightly together but her voice was steady.

"Oh?" He sounded puzzled.

"I'm not going to do that penance at all," Sister Joan said. "You had no right to hear my confession in the first place. You're not an ordained priest."

"That's a very foolish thing to say, Sister Joan." He sounded as if he were mildly disappointed in her.

"Perhaps." She took a step forward. "Twenty years ago you were arrested for causing damage to the trees on the Tarquin estate and Mrs Fairly identified you. You were found guilty, weren't you? Did they recommend psychiatric treatment?"

"They didn't understand," he said. "They didn't appreciate that it was my duty to punish — they tried to make me believe that I was mentally unbalanced. I am not, of course, but they didn't understand. Twenty years of in and out, in and out, one hospital after another, and nobody understood. There was no peace for me save in the cloister. It took years for me to reach that conclusion but when I did — oh, I became a model patient. I was released five years ago and I went north. I decided to train for the priesthood, you see. That would give me the authority I required to impose penance upon sinners. But it wasn't any use. After only eighteen months they rejected me as unsuitable. Can you imagine that? They knew nothing of my background or my true history but they rejected me. Temperamentally unsuitable, Father Superior said. But he offered me a consolation prize. Oh, he very generously offered me a consolation prize. I could work at the seminary, do odd jobs, chop wood — that was very satisfying for me to see the splinters fly and the wood bleed sap."

"You knew Father Timothy?"

"He had a late vocation as I did. Yes, I have a vocation whatever they might say! He was a nice person, rather shy and quiet, having to take insulin injections for his diabetes. He was a nice person. They let him become a priest, ordained him. Then he told me he was coming down here, to take over from Father Malone, coming to this very place where that bitch had identified me all those years ago! I had to come in his place, Sister. I came to pronounce sentence and to execute judgement. Oh, I had no thought of killing her. Not then."

"But you killed Father Timothy."

"It was an unfortunate necessity. I bore him no grudge. Father Philip escorted him to the station."

"But not on to the train?"

"Father Philip wished to get back to the seminary so he parted from Father Timothy and went away. I was in the tunnel where the old siding runs. All I had to do was beckon Father Timothy just before he went on to the platform and he came across to me. I told him that I had a surprise for him. The first blow killed him. It wasn't my intention to make him suffer at all. I was only wearing a raincoat and the instant he fell I stripped it off, stripped the body and then — it was very necessary that he shouldn't be recognized, you see."

"And nobody saw anything at all?"

"Why should they? The tunnel curves round along by the old disused bit of track. I washed my hands and the blade of the axe in the conduit — the water flows fast there, and it only took a few moments to change clothes with him, and then later to roll up the axe in the raincoat and put them into my suitcase. I waited until it was darker before I got a luggage trolley and wheeled the body further down the track. There were no railway officials about. There seldom are these days, you know. When the next train came in I simply boarded it. Very simple indeed."

"Yes," Sister Joan said.

"I nearly didn't kill Mrs Fairly," he was continuing. "She had done her penance for betraying me, with her husband dying and no children to carry on his name. I really did intend to spare her. After all it was twenty years ago and I've changed very much during the intervening years. Yes, I intended to spare her, but it wasn't any use. She kept looking at me, looking as if she were trying to remember. I knew it was only a matter of time. And there wasn't any time. I had to act very swiftly. When Father Stephens invited me to accompany him on a late evening walk I went back for my coat. I'd been right to be cautious. Mrs Fairly was on the telephone in the study, making an appointment to meet with someone. I had the tablets — my own supply of Valium — already crushed up. I'd noticed that she took sugar in her tea and Father Stephens didn't, so I merely emptied the tablets into the sugar bowl. One has to be prepared at all times for every eventuality. Not that I expected her to drink all the tea! Sufficient to make her a little dizzy would suit me very well. I rejoined Father Stephens and we took our walk but the weather threatened storm so we came in quite soon. Mrs Fairly was just going upstairs with her tea tray. Father Stephens made a jesting comment, enquiring if she had had her tipple. We went upstairs almost at once. I waited about fifteen minutes, then went into Mrs Fairly's room. She had drunk some of the tea and clearly noticed the odd taste because she was sitting up in her bed, grimacing, looking into her cup. I had Father Timothy's syringe with me and all I had to do was grab her wrist and inject. She went into convulsions almost immediately. Fortunately Father Stephens had switched on his radio and I could hear the strains of music coming from his room. He heard nothing."

"You took the handbag?"

"I snatched it up because it occurred to me that Mrs Fairly had very likely kept any clippings relating to the case. It was probably the most exciting thing that had happened to her in her entire life! There wasn't time to look carefully — I feared Father Stephens might leave his room to visit the toilet or something, so I took it to my room and had a cursory glance inside it, but I was feeling rather tired by then. Killing someone is rather exhausting, you know, so I wrapped it round in brown paper and popped it into the refuse bin. That was early the next morning before I went up to the convent to offer mass. I would have put it back in Mrs Fairly's room but Father Stephens was up and about and the opportunity didn't arise."

"You damaged the tree at the convent," Sister Joan said.

It was important to keep him talking, to keep the words flowing out of him in a long stream of self-justification.

"Very early on the morning that I arrived. I caught the overnight train and walked up to the convent. That was my first task, you see. To wreak vengeance on the wood. I left my luggage down at the station, then walked back to town and sat in the waiting-room. I didn't want to interrupt Father Malone's leavetaking."

"And after Mrs Fairly died?"

"Oh, I hoped that would be the end of it," he said. "I had my parish duties to fulfil. But no action exists in isolation, does it? Mrs Fairly had been talking on the telephone to somebody. It might have been her niece. And her niece was coming here. She might enquire about the handbag. She might enquire about me!" He sounded aggrieved at the possibility.

"Mrs Fairly's niece was killed on the train," Sister Joan said.

"Oh, that was easy enough." In the uncertain light he seemed to be smiling. "I got a lift to the next station and when the train came I ran along looking for the young woman who resembled the schoolgirl in the photograph in Mrs Fairly's room. I have a much better memory for faces than most people. She was on her own in a compartment and I opened the door and asked her if she was Mrs Fairly's niece. She said she was and I simply boarded the train. She'd no suspicions of a priest at all. She even bent down to get a handkerchief out of her bag and I only needed to give her one blow. The train did the rest when I opened the door and thrust her out. That was quite dangerous. I almost fell out myself, but God protects His own. I alighted from the train when it reached Bodmin and resumed my waiting on the platform. I was extremely fortunate because she was on the earlier train. I might have had to look for her on the later ones, and then someone might have noticed me.

"And Stephanie Hugh?" She spoke carefully, quietly.

"They kept on coming, you see." He spoke peevishly. "First the niece and then her friend. I couldn't be sure. The niece might have mentioned the aunt's phone call to her friend and the friend would start asking questions. And I had no idea what she looked like, no idea at all! Then I hit upon rather a neat scheme. Father Stephens had jotted down her telephone number so I simply rang her up and asked her to come down on an earlier train. I was due to take the confirmation class in the afternoon so I was cutting it very fine, but I met her at the station and suggested the short cut through the walkway. It leads to the car-park."

"Where you put her in the boot of the convent car."

"Another stroke of luck! The lay sister Sister Jerome was just walking away from it as we emerged from the walkway. I had meant to deliver the blow there, but Miss Hugh was quite a hefty looking young woman. I said to her, 'Ah! Sister promised to leave me some of her potted jam in the boot,' and we went over. The boot was unlocked. We bent over and — oh, it was very swift and clean. Not a soul to see me and God helping me every step of the way!"

"And then you went off to the confirmation class?" It was difficult to keep the horrified disbelief out of her voice.

"I must carry out my parish duties," he said primly. "The deaths were an unhappy necessity. Even you must see that, Sister. And it hasn't been easy for me — having to settle into the routine of parochial life and track down these women and then there was the syringe to be buried."

"You didn't bury the axe," Sister Joan said.

"I meant to do so, but then I saw Sister Jerome in her place when I was officiating at the early mass. She was the nun I'd seen walking away from the car. I waited until the sisters had left the chapel and gone to breakfast and then I put the axe under her seat. I had wiped it very carefully first, of course, and brought it with me in my bag along with my vestments and stole. I was always very neat."

"But why do you damage trees and plants anyway?" she asked, bewilderment almost overcoming her fear. "What harm did they ever do you?"

"They don't do penance," he said tightly. "Have you never noticed, Sister, that in the season of Lent when the world prepares to mourn the death of Our Lord the plants start to spring up in defiance. Flowers, bushes, trees, all springing into life, not caring that Good Friday is on the way? Everything must do penance, you know. We can't make exceptions."

He had neither axe nor syringe but he must have something else or he'd not have spoken so freely.

"They do know about you," she said.

"The police are making enquiries at the seminary. Father Timothy will be identified, you know. You may have killed him, taken his clothes, brought his suitcase along with your own, but he'll be identified, probably has been already. And you're not a diabetic, are you? The man who died was and that only applies to Father Timothy."

"Oh, the police are very clever," he agreed. "They found the handbag and put a box in its place. I really thought you were the one who'd done that, Sister. I suspected you of setting a trap for me of some kind. However it makes no difference. I must continue with my work until the last possible moment. The whole world must be brought to penance."

Yes, he had something else. Against the dark cloth of his garments she caught a glimpse of a long, thin blade.

"They will lock you up for the rest of your life," she said. "They won't accept the reasons you give. I don't accept them! You destroy things because it gives you pleasure and that has nothing to do with being good. It has everything to do with being evil and cruel. So don't try to force me to do what you're pleased to call penance. You don't know the first thing about it!"

She had raised her voice, partly because she was shivering with nervous excitement and needed to assert herself, partly because she had sensed rather than seen a slight movement at the back of the church, more a shifting of the darkness than anything.

"You be quiet!" he ordered thickly. "Do your penance. I ordered you to — "

"Sorry, but you've no authority to order me to do anything." She tensed herself, preparing to fling herself sideways if he leapt forwards. "You've no authority over anyone or anything. You can't damage all the trees in the world or kill all the people who might remember you. You've failed before you've even begun."

"How dare you speak to me like that?" His voice was low, thin and sharp as the blade of the knife he was holding. "Have you no respect for the priesthood?"

"Every respect," she said scornfully, "but you're no priest. Dressing up in another man's clothes can't turn you into

328

another person. That makes you stupid, and I've no respect for that either. So you stay here and play your sick little games. I don't have to take any notice of you."

The darkness split into shadows and she flung herself aside as the sharp point of light that was the tip of the blade glittered downwards and at the same instant every light in the church was switched on, dazzling them in its radiance.

She had landed heavily at the side of the altar, wedged between steps and the door of the sacristy. John Moore was struggling in the grip of two policemen, his face contorted, unintelligible sounds hissing from his mouth. The knife arched towards the floor and stuck, quivering, in the thick pad of a kneeling hassock.

Sister Joan stayed where she was, uneasily aware that if she took any action she would burst into a flood of hysterical tears.

"Are you all right, Sister?" Detective Sergeant Mill had emerged from the confessional at the back of the church and walked up the side aisle to where she crouched.

"Yes. Yes, I think so." She dragged her gaze from the figure being frogmarched towards the main doors. "Yes, I'll be fine. Just don't talk to me for a few moments."

"When you're ready, Sister," he said, "I think we could both do with a strong cup of tea, don't you?"

"Yes. Yes, of course." She pulled herself up, smoothing down her habit, grateful for his brisk, impersonal tone that had defused her growing hysteria. "I'll see to it right away."

And not forgetting to genuflect, albeit shakily, to the altar, she went back via the sacristy into the house.

16

"ONE would like to know the exact sequence of events," Mother Dorothy said. She was seated on the hardest chair she could find in the presbytery parlour. Father Stephens and Detective Sergeant Mill occupied the sofa and Sister Joan sat, after an approving nod from her superior, in the armchair, her foot on a hassock. Sister Perpetua, who had just diagnosed a sprain and bandaged it, sat on the arm of the second armchair. Outside the pale February sun shone on the few brave bulbs struggling up into the despoiled border.

"John Moore was an orphan, a difficult child, moved from one foster home to the next," Detective Sergeant Mill said. "By the time he was in his late teens he had already been placed on probation for petty theft and disturbing the peace. He had also begun to develop religious mania though nobody realized it at that stage. Mrs Fairly used to go up to the Tarquin house to help out with the cooking there and saw him hanging around just about the time the trees were vandalized. So she was able to identify him and was always rather proud of helping the police. I reckon that was why she kept the cutting. Anyway, twenty years passed. Moore had moved north, had tried several times to enter holy orders but without success, and was in the right place as far as he was concerned when a request was sent to the seminary for someone to replace Father Malone during his sabbatical. Father Timothy had been a late vocation, nearing thirty, a diabetic and a man of great compassion. He befriended Moore, which meant that he was quite unsuspicious when the latter waved to him and beckoned him into the railway siding."

"Where he was killed," Sister Perpetua said.

"With one blow of the axe. Moore wore nothing under his raincoat so he quickly stripped the body, put on the priest's clothes, on which I've no doubt we'll find a blood spot or two, rolled up the raincoat and put it with the axe in his own suitcase. He'd done his best to render the body unidentifiable before then, but you don't want those details. He then boarded the next train, carrying both suitcases, made his way here, left the cases down at the station and walked up to the convent with the axe under his coat. He damaged the trees — partly to get rid of his manic energy, I think. Destruction and damage gave him the kind of thrill another man might get from sexual intercourse, if you'll excuse me, ladies?"

"We have heard about sex in the convent," Mother Dorothy said crisply.

"Yes, of course. Anyway he returned to the station and sat in the waiting-room until he'd seen Father Malone's train depart. He'd heard that Father Malone was an experienced pastor and a very shrewd judge of people so he decided not to risk meeting him. Instead he gave you, Sister, the impression he'd just arrived and you took him along to the presbytery."

"But surely she might have recognized him?" Sister Joan interjected.

"It was certainly a risk but even if she had, so what? She'd identified a teenage tearaway. In twenty years people can change."

"St Francis of Assisi is an example of that," Sister Perpetua said.

"Whether she recognized him or not we'll never know," Detective Sergeant Mill said. "The fact she dug out that old cutting suggests that she was perhaps puzzled by some feeling of familiarity. Evidently she was interrupted while looking at it because she slipped it into the pages of the Account book. She telephoned you, Sister, asking for a meeting. Moore had slipped back to get his coat having set out on a brisk stroll with Father Stephens. He says now that he believed she had recognized him, but since he had used his own stock of Valium to crush up already my own view is that he intended to kill her all along. Her being on the telephone simply gave him the chance to slip into the kitchen and mix the tablets with the sugar."

"Then he gave her time to drink some of the tea, went in and injected her with the insulin from Father Timothy's suitcase, emptied out all but the dregs of the tea and — did she keep her Valium by the bed?" Sister Joan looked at him.

"He merely emptied out the tablets and flushed them down the toilet. He took her handbag, intending to search it later for anything she'd kept concerning that earlier affair, but he could hear Father Stephens moving about in his room so he wrapped the bag in brown paper and early the next morning pushed it into the bin."

"Meaning to take it out later and have a closer look," Father Stephens said.

"It was his bad luck that Sister Joan was sent here to fill in as housekeeper. Sister Joan insisted that Mrs Fairly would never have committed suicide and that made us look more closely at everything."

"Sister Joan," said Mother Dorothy, "has her uses."

"That wasn't the end of it for Moore," he continued. "There was the possibility that Mrs Fairly had been speaking to her niece over the telephone and so Sylvia Potter had to be removed. He cut short his confirmation class, hitched a lift to the next station — we're enquiring into that now — picked her out on the train and entered the compartment. He had the devil's own luck, begging your pardon, Mother Dorothy."

"We've heard of the Devil at the convent too," Mother Dorothy assured him.

"Sylvia Potter was in one of the old-style closed carriages and alone, so he hit her over the head, pushed her out, alighted himself at the station and resumed his apparent waiting for her."

"He was pacing the platform," Sister Joan said.

"Having just alighted from the previous train. And then came word that Miss Potter's friend was on her way. By that time I don't believe he thought of it as a risk but as an opportunity to kill again. He'd moved past trees and plants, you see. So he phoned up Miss Hugh and asked her to come by the early train, met her at the station, and suggested they take the short cut through the walkway that leads to the car-park. He meant to kill her there but then he noticed Sister Jerome walking away from the convent car so he made an excuse to Miss Hugh and she went unsuspectingly to the boot, expecting to find jars of jam there, poor girl! One blow and she was inside the boot and he walked calmly away, merely a priest going about his business."

"And I came down to the station later to meet Miss Hugh," Sister Joan said.

"And ran into Petrie who got the message regarding the body in the car boot. John Moore must have started to fancy himself safe, safe enough to leave the axe in the convent chapel and bury the syringe there. The bloodstained raincoat wasn't far off by the way. We were closing in on him."

"And he'd found the empty box I'd put in the refuse bin in place of the handbag," Sister Joan reflected.

"A somewhat unwise course of action," he said.

"If you're looking for wisdom," Sister Perpetua advised, "don't apply to Sister Joan. Other qualities she has in plenty."

"When you came round last evening you said all that about the police finding the handbag to throw him off my scent, didn't you?" Sister Joan said.

"I was waiting for back-up before I

arrested him on suspicion of murder," he nodded. "I couldn't be sure what other weapons he might have on him and I felt it more prudent to wait until he was out of the presbytery. Anyway the back-up arrived and since he'd mentioned that he'd be praying in the church we waited in there. I was a trifle alarmed when Sister Joan trotted in. There was no time to warn her to leave at once because Moore came in. After that I played it literally by ear. And Sister Joan goaded him into telling her the whole story."

"I'd already guessed bits of it," Sister Joan explained.

"What alerted you in the first place?" Mother Dorothy looked at her attentively.

"Nothing until near the end, Mother Dorothy. Then someone, Father Stephens it was, mentioned that Father Timothy probably had an unfortunate manner because he was all alone in the world with no friends or relatives."

"He had mentioned the fact to me," Father Stephens said.

"But Father Malone told me when he was leaving that Father Timothy had relatives in Falmouth and would probably stay the night there before continuing on down here. I'd forgotten all about that. I suppose they mentioned it when Father Malone heard from the seminary they were sending a replacement for him."

"He didn't mention that to me. He did make all the arrangements for his successor though, wishing to spare me any extra trouble. And, of course, I'd no reason to phone the seminary myself. Father — I mean John Moore, said he was going to ring them."

"But never did." Detective Sergeant Mill uncoiled his long legs and stood up. "I reckon he'll be diagnosed as unfit to plead. He seems to have gone completely over the top now. You were very fortunate to escape injury, Sister Joan."

"Yes, I know." She spoke thoughtfully.

"So that seems to be that. I wanted to put you fully in the picture. Now I've a report to write. I'll see myself out, Father. Sisters."

He went out, closing the door gently. The sound of the front door closing was like the end of a chapter.

"And we must be returning to the

convent too," Mother Dorothy said. "Father, you have not yet acquired a new housekeeper?"

"I'm afraid not, Reverend Mother."

"Our new lay sister is not settling as happily as I could wish," Mother Dorothy said. "I asked her if she would be willing to work as housekeeper here at the presbytery if you weren't yet suited and she intimated that she would. Sister Jerome is very competent and an excellent cook and will enjoy the work, I'm sure. Will it suit you if I send Sister Perpetua down with her later?"

"That's most kind of you, Mother Dorothy," he said fervently. "With no relief cleric I am going to be pretty busy these next months, far too busy to break in a laywoman to the routine of a priest. I shall welcome Sister Jerome with open arms."

"Metaphorically speaking, I hope," Mother Dorothy said dryly. "Sister Joan, have you packed your things?"

"Yes, Mother Dorothy."

"Sister Perpetua will get your suitcase. We came in a taxi this morning since the police have not yet released our own car so we shall return in a taxi. I hope the circumstances justify the extravagance, though I must point out to you, Sister Joan, that if you hadn't exposed yourself to such danger you would not now be nursing a badly sprained ankle and we could all have had a nice, brisk walk back over the moor."

"Yes, Mother." Sister Joan pulled herself to her feet and tested her weight on her foot gingerly. "Mother, about Sister Jerome, Mrs Fairly thought she had remembered something about her. That was why she telephoned me to ask for a meeting."

"She probably remembered that Sister Jerome spent three years in gaol for what is termed a mercy killing but is no less murder before a suicide note left by her mother was found. Sister Jerome had concealed it rather than have the shame of self-slaughter attached to her mother's memory. She was already a professed nun when the affair occurred and there was some publicity at the time. I daresay Mrs Fairly recalled the name and that led to her phoning you."

"Sister Jerome went to prison?" Sister

Joan stared at her superior.

"For a crime she didn't commit," Mother Dorothy said. "She had been given leave of absence from her convent to care for her mother who was terminally ill. She nobly and foolishly took the blame when her mother was found dead from an overdose. When the truth came out she was released immediately, of course. She could have returned to her old Order but she craved anonymity and applied to our London House, where she was accepted."

"You knew this when she came to us?" Sister Joan asked.

"You think I ought to have informed the entire community? Our past lives are past when we enter the religious life, Sister. What happened to Sister Jerome was nobody else's business. I am telling you now so that you may understand a little more fully why her insistence on penance does have a cause. She blames herself for her mother's suicide. It was Sister Jerome who went through the clippings you are collecting up in the storeroom. Sister David mentioned it to me and I asked Sister Jerome if she knew anything about it. She had been fearful lest some item about her might have been preserved, though it happened up north."

"Then how did Mrs Fairly remember it?"

"Mrs Fairly was involved with a group fighting against legalized euthanasia some years ago. Naturally they followed news of such cases with interest and Sister Jerome's name did appear in the papers."

"Poor Sister Jerome," Sister Perpetua said. "A very difficult character."

"She will make an excellent housekeeper," Mother Dorothy said firmly. "She will keep Father Stephens anchored within the realms of reality and Father Malone, when he returns, will advise her about the quite unnecessary guilt she still feels."

"Father Stephens," said Sister Joan, limping out to the taxi which had just drawn up outside, "is a nice young man."

In the background Father Stephens gave a slight cough, remarking wryly, "It does us all good to be talked about as if we were not here."

"In your case," said Mother Dorothy,

eyes twinkling behind her spectacles, "quite a lot of good, Father! You were most helpful to Sister Joan when she was here, I'm sure. You will be equally helpful to Sister Jerome. Try to show her there is still some joy in life and that constantly punishing ourselves can become an indulgence."

"Regarding which — " His face had flushed with sudden anxiety. "Since John Moore was no priest the masses he offered, the confessions he heard, were invalid. I will have to inform the congregation of the facts as soon as possible. He knew the liturgy backwards."

"So does the Devil," Sister Perpetua said. "It's knowing it right way up that counts. I'll drive down straight after lunch with Sister Jerome."

In the taxi Sister Joan sat with her foot stuck out in front of her. Her ankle hurt and she felt a sudden gloom descend upon her spirits.

"Looking forward to going home, Sister?" Mother Dorothy glanced at her.

"Yes, Mother," she said obediently.

But do I? Inexorably her mind questioned. When I was at the presbytery there was a sense of freedom, of being my own mistress again, of being involved in the world. Yet I missed the convent, the quiet routine, the rest of the community. Am I turning into one of those dreadful people who are only happy in the place where they are not?

"We shall pay off the taxi and walk the rest of the way," Mother Dorothy said as the convent gates hove into view. "Can you manage, Sister?"

"Yes, I think so."

Under the gaze of the taxi driver she struggled out of the vehicle and set her foot on the ground. It throbbed but was less painful than before.

"I can manage fine, Mother Dorothy," she assured her. "I'll look on it as an extra bit of penance."

"One moment!" Mother Dorothy held up her hand. "Driver, take Sister Joan all the way to the back door, will you? In you get again, Sister! I'll speak to you later. Come along, Sister Perpetua!"

Sister Joan sat in solitary state as the taxi proceeded up the drive. She knew only too well what Mother Dorothy would be saying to her later.

"Penance isn't a label we wear to trumpet forth our sanctity, Sister. Even less do we announce our penitential practices in front of other people."

"This do you, Sister?" The driver turned his head to enquire as they reached the yard.

"Thank you, yes. This is fine."

"Bit of a tartar, isn't she?" He jerked his head back.

"A lot of a tartar," Sister Joan said, and found herself laughing as the taxi backed away, and Sister Gabrielle, cloak over her shoulders, came to the kitchen door with Alice gambolling at her heels.

"So you're home again, girl," she observed. "No doubt the quality of the cooking will drop into the nether regions, but since it's Lent we may as well put up with it. You'd better come in. Tell us what you've been up to. Nothing to your credit, I'll be bound!"

"Not much to my credit," Sister Joan said ruefully. "But I'll tell you something, Sister Gabrielle, suddenly it feels wonderful to be home!"